D0248638

PERMANENTLY WITHDRAWN
FROM
HAMMERSMITH AND FULHAM
PUBLIC LIBRARIES

WAFER

WAFER

Is it real
or is it
EMPTY?

Ha! Ha!

Take a lucky guess!

EMPTY!
Yum.

A TINY BIT
LUCKY
BY Liz Pichon
(who's well lucky)

Scholastic Children's Books
An imprint of Scholastic Ltd
Euston House, 24 Eversholt Street
London, NW1 1DB, UK

Registered office: Westfield Road,
Southam, Warwickshire, CV47 0RA
SCHOLASTIC and associated logos are trademarks
and/or registered trademarks of Scholastic Inc.

Copyright © Liz Pichon, 2014
The right of Liz Pichon to be identified
as the author and illustrator
of this work has been asserted by her.

Trade ISBN 978 1 407138 87 9
Non-Trade ISBN 978 1 407152 28 8

A CIP catalogue record for this book is
available from the British Library.

All rights reserved.
This book is sold subject to the condition
that it shall not, by way of trade or otherwise,
be lent, hired our or otherwise circulated in
any form of binding or cover other than that
in which it is published. No part of this publication may
be reproduced, stored in a retrieval system, or transmitted in
any form or by any means (electronic, mechanical, photocopying,
recording or otherwise) without the prior written permission
of Scholastic Limited.

Printed and bound by CPI Group (UK) Ltd, Croydon, CR0 4YY
Papers used by Scholastic Children's Books are made
from wood grown in sustainable forests.

1 3 5 7 9 10 8 6 4 2

This is a work of fiction. Names, characters, places, incidents and dialogues are
products of the author's imagination or are used fictitiously. Any resemblance
to actual people, living or dead, events or locales is entirely coincidental.

www.scholastic.co.uk

To Judith. Thanks for all your support x
Hey girl! Zoe, expert editor x
VERY much
SO much
Loads
Massive thanks
Thank-You METER

My To Do List
- Do homework ✓
- Do doodle ✓
- Eat wafer ✓

According to my dad ...

THIS bit of string ...

is going to be ... a kite.

(Really?)

It doesn't look much like a KITE to me?

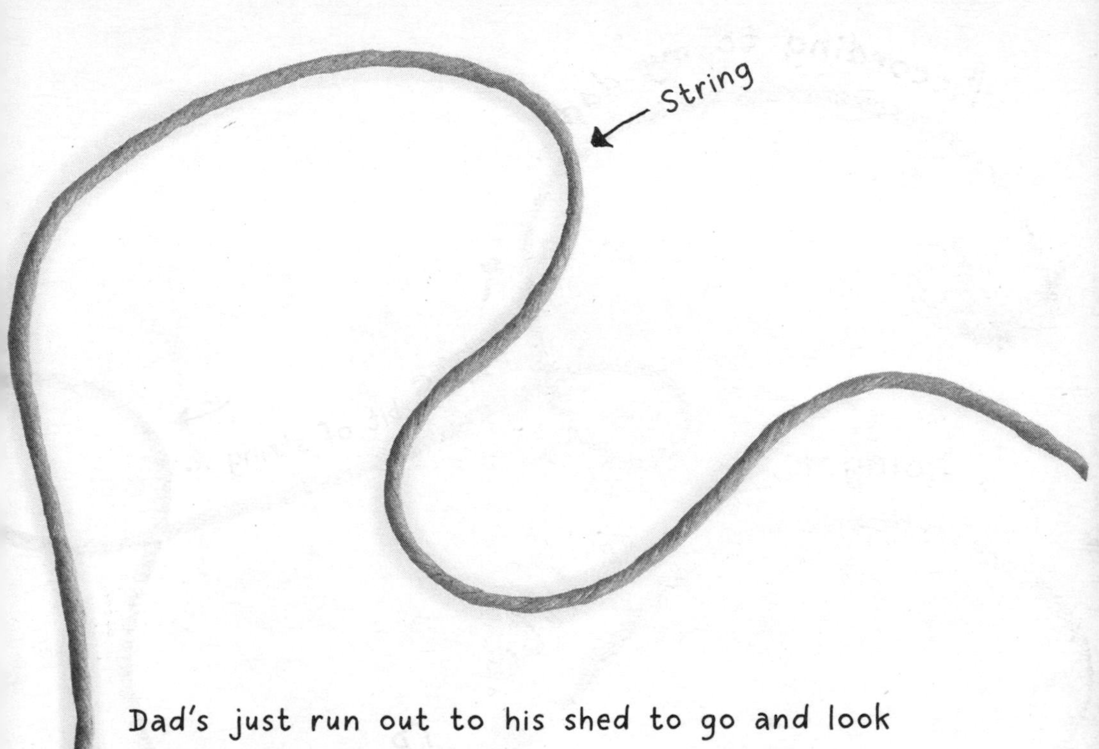

Dad's just run out to his shed to go and look for an even l o n g e r piece of string. He's been gone for a while now. I thought about turning the TV back on?

But instead, I did THIS...

LOOK!
It's a string doodle.
(A snail, in case you were wondering.)

Here's another one...
How about I add
some drawing.

Brilliant! (If I do say so myself.)

Who knew string could be so useful?

(Apart from my Granny Mavis, of course.)

The NEXT time I'm in a lesson that gets a bit **dull** (which happens), I'm going to bring out my EMERGENCY piece of STRING and make a few doodles.

That way it'll look like I'm REALLY busy.

When Dad comes back from the shed he's SMILING and holding up ... ANOTHER piece of string.

"Here we go, Tom, this is PERFECT."

I'm looking at the string thinking – it's exactly the same as the OTHER bit?

"That's great, Dad," I say, trying to sound enthusiastic (and failing).

NORMALLY I LOVE making things (like my string doodles). But Dad came and interrupted me when I was RIGHT in the middle of watching

the BEST cartoon show EVER.

He stood in front of the TV and started shaking his head in a disapproving kind of way.

"TOM, why are you stuck inside watching TV when it's SUCH a lovely day?" he wanted to know.

Firstly – it was NOT a lovely day. It was damp and cold.

Secondly – I was watching TV because

THE CRAZY FRUIT BUNCH was on and it's

But I didn't say that. I just kept my EYES fixed on the TV screen and shrugged.

There are SO many things you could be doing instead of STARING at a screen. Come on, TOM, turn off the TV.

"Aww, Dad! That's not FAIR. Can't I just finish watching my cartoon?" I asked him.

"Honestly, Tom, when I was your age, I was ALWAYS outside running about in the fresh air. I hardly EVER watched TV," he told me proudly.

"That's because TV hadn't been invented when you were my age, Dad."

(He is quite old, after all.)

"Of course  had been invented!

I just liked playing outside. Climbing trees and making things with twigs ... that kind of thing."

"What sort of things did you make with TWIGS?" I wanted to know.

"I made LOTS of things."

"Like WHAT?" I asked.

"You know, TWIG things. Things made out of TWIGS. Anyway, it doesn't matter what I made. The main thing was I was OUT in the fresh air having FUN."

"Playing with twigs doesn't sound like much fun to me," I told Dad.

"There are PLENTY of other things you can do outside. You can play in the garden, for a start."

"It's too cold."

"So run around! Or you could ask Derek over?"

(I shook my head because I knew Derek was busy.)

"He's at a friend's house – probably watching TV," I said, trying to make a point.

(I knew he wasn't – but that didn't matter.)

Derek being busy

HOW about inviting your NEW neighbour June over? I'm sure she'd come round to play if you asked her.

(Well *that* wasn't going to happen.) 

"Dad, it's not like I'm **FOUR** years old, my friends don't come round to play any more – well, not unless we're having a band practice."

(I DEFINITELY wasn't going to be asking June over.)

Since she moved in next door, June's not exactly been that friendly to me.

It's bad enough having her CAT wandering around OUR garden AND she's in my class at school too.

Every time she sees me (which is a lot, because she sits next to AMY PORTER, who sits next to me),

June thinks it's FUNNY to say,

"TOM ... you do realize that DUDE3 are actually a RUBBISH band."

Which is NOT TRUE and also REALLY ANNOYING.

If I had an ANNOYING METER, June would be about

Sometimes there's not much to choose between them.

When Mum came in to see what Dad and I were chatting about ...

she JOINED IN!

"You're not watching  again, are you, Tom?" she asked me.

"I'm TRYING to watch TV," I told her while *leaning* to the side of Dad.

It's not like I watch TELLY all the time.

I just LOVE THE CRAZY FRUIT BUNCH.

The chances of me being able to watch the rest of the cartoon were disappearing FAST.

It was impossible to concentrate with BOTH Mum and Dad GLARING at me.

So I GAVE UP - and I turned it off myself.

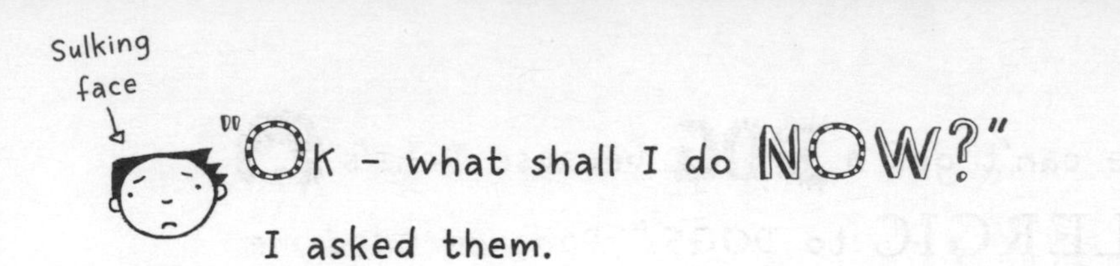

"Ok – what shall I do NOW?"

I asked them.

"Well, there are LOADS of other things we could do."

"Like WHAT?"

"How about ... we go for a walk?" Dad suggested.

"A WALK – where to?" I wanted to know.

"Somewhere NICE," he said.

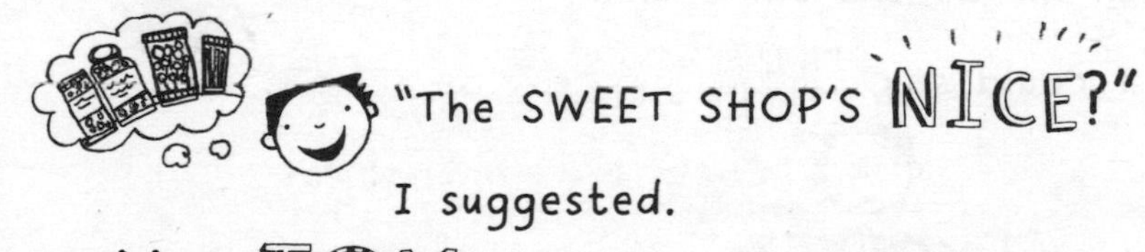

"The SWEET SHOP'S NICE?"

I suggested.

"No, TOM, I meant somewhere like the park."

"If we had a DOG I'd be REALLY HAPPY to go out for walks all the time," I told Dad.

"We can't get a DOG because Delia's ALLERGIC to DOGS," Dad reminded me.

So I said quietly,

Dad didn't hear me because he was busy picking up a bit of string that was on the shelf.

"I KNOW, how about I show you how to make a KITE? Then we can fly it together AND get some fresh air at the same time!"

Before I could say, "MAYBE?" or

"Could we do that later?"

Mum got all EXCITED and said,

"That's a BRILLIANT IDEA!"

(It was an OK idea. I'd still rather watch the rest of

"COME on, it will be FUN,"

Dad said, trying to convince me.

And THAT'S when he disappeared into his shed to go and find ANOTHER piece of string.

Mum went to the kitchen and came back with: some plastic bags ... a couple of bin liners ... and a roll of sticky tape.

"These might be useful?"

Mum's got a thing about plastic bags and bin liners, she uses them for EVERYTHING.

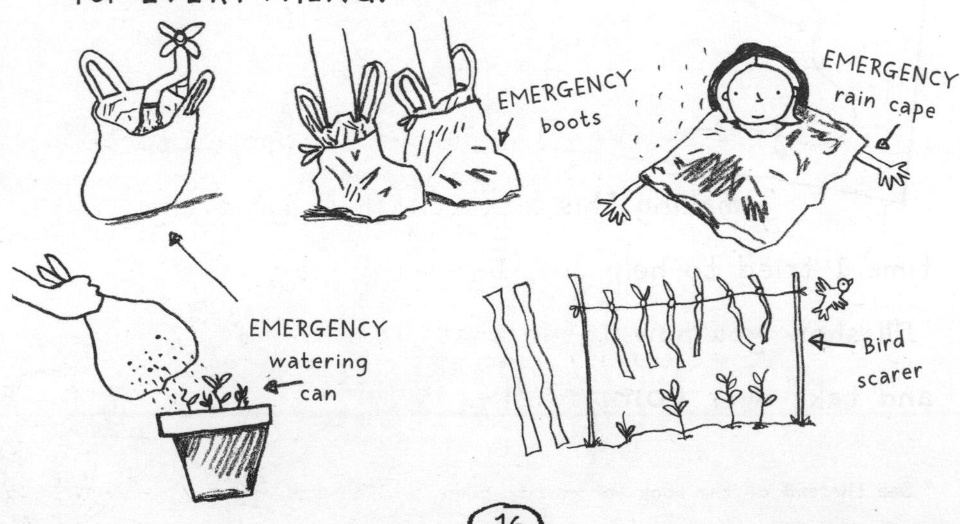

When Dad saw the plastic bags he said they were

perfect!

"Perfect for what?" I wondered.

"All we need now are couple of sticks and some scissors," Dad told me. Then he got some paper and drew out how we were going to make the kite.*

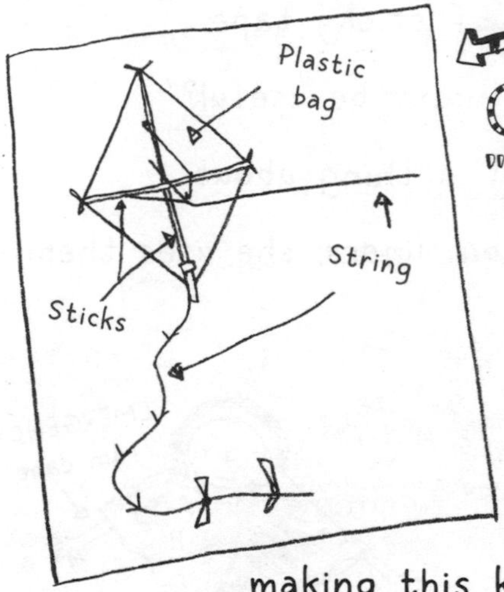

Plastic bag

String

Sticks

OK, I kind of get it now.

"Let's go to my shed and finish making the kite there," Dad said.

So we did.

We were supposed to be making this kite together. But every time I tried to help out, Dad would say, "I'll show you how to do that, Tom," and take over **completely**.

* See the end of the book for how to make a KITE.

"LOOK, WE'VE MADE IT!" Dad said.

(HE'D made it - but I didn't say that.)

"Shall we go and fly it?"

Dad suggested.

"What, NOW?"

"YES now - get your coat on, Tom, and let's go."

(Like I had a choice.)

When we came back into the house, Delia was in the kitchen. Lately she's been going out a lot with her friends, so I haven't seen much of her.

It's been

She was looking at her phone (as usual).

Dad said, "Look what we've made, Delia."

(Well - DAD made it - but I didn't tell her that.)

Delia said,

not even looking up.

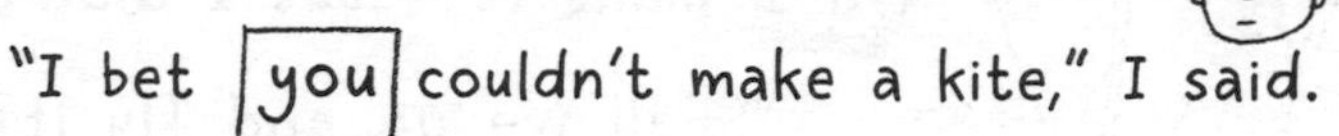

"I bet you couldn't make a kite," I said.

"You're right. It's a life skill that's passed me by."

Mum says, "Well done, Tom. See what you can do when you don't watch TV?"

Delia adds, but I'm not sure she really means it.

Dad and I get our coats and set off for the park. He's holding the kite really carefully so it doesn't get tangled.

"The BEST place to catch the WIND is up on the hill," Dad says. "There's a real KNACK to launching a KITE, Tom."

"Yes, Dad."

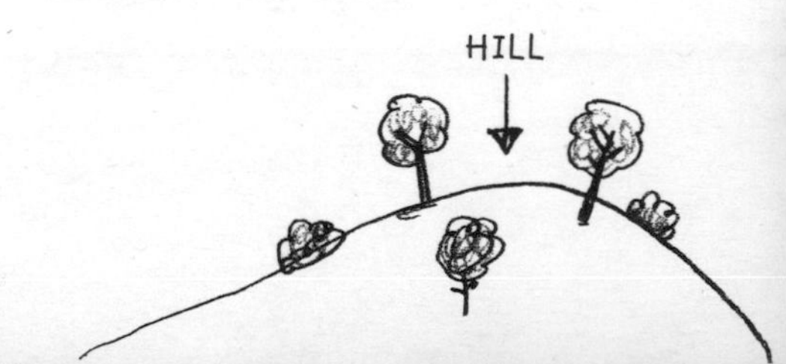

When we get to the hill, Dad checks the string is nice and tight. Then he shows me exactly where to run and HOW to LAUNCH the kite up in the air. It all seems easy enough. So we give it a go.

But the kite keeps sinking down like a stone.

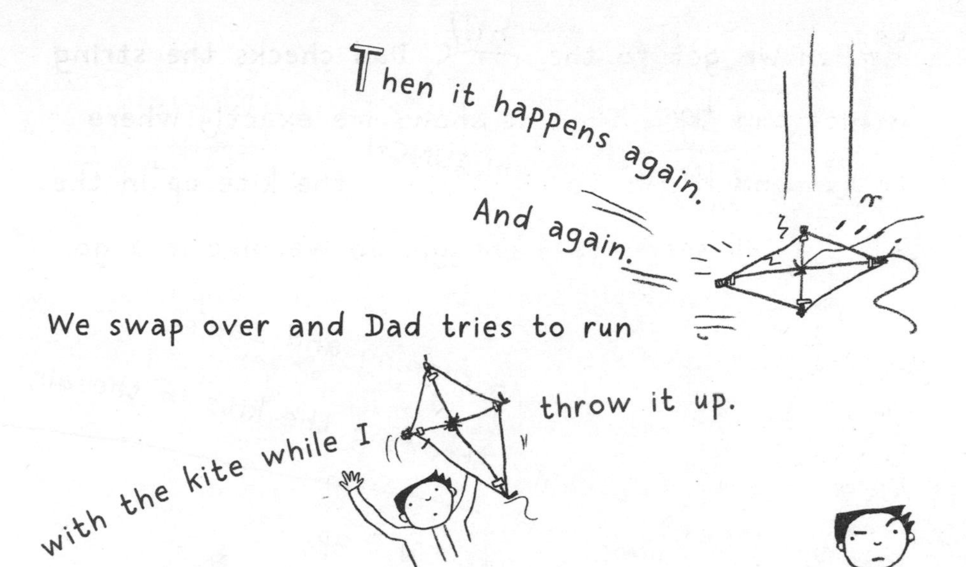

Then it happens again.

And again.

We swap over and Dad tries to run with the kite while I throw it up.

Then I recognize someone who's walking towards me with a very tiny little dog.

It's only MARCUS MELDREW.

If there was ONE person I wouldn't want to bump into right now – it would be Marcus. I bet he's going to make comments about my kite. (Groan.)

I can't really ignore him so I'm forced to say hello.

"Hi, Tom, what's that?"

(Here we go.)

"It's a KITE."

"WHAT? THAT THING made from plastic bags is a kite?"

"YES, Marcus, it's a kite. My dad made it and I sort of helped. It FLIES really well.

In fact, it's AMAZING."

"That ⇨ kite can actually fly in the air?" Marcus says, sounding surprised.

Dad comes to pick up the kite and says "Hello, Marcus" then walks back up the hill to have another go. I don't really want Marcus to stay and WATCH.

Especially as I've just told him how good it is.

"Ready when you are, Tom!"

Dad shouts.

(Oh, great.)

"Bye, Marcus," I say to him,

hoping he'll GO.

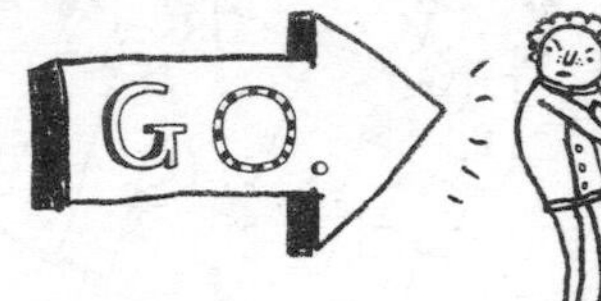

"I'm not going anywhere, I want to see this AMAZING kite fly," Marcus says.

(Annoyingly.)

"OK, you will," I tell him while thinking

PLEASE FLY, PLEASE FLY.

Marcus takes out a half-eaten sandwich from his pocket and starts to EAT it, like he's at the CINEMA or watching a show.

"READY, Dad!" I shout. "I'll throw the kite UP and you PULL it and RUN at the same time."

That's the plan.

(So far this plan hasn't worked.)

I'm cheering and saying,

"YES, IT'S **FLYING, IT'S** FLYING!"

Dad pulls the string to keep it in the sky.

"It **works!** It's flying! **HOORAY!**"

Marcus has his MOUTH open like he can't believe what he's seeing.

(He's not the only one!)

"I told you it flies," I say, when Marcus's little dog runs past me and LEAPS into the air. And I say "NO!" thinking he's about to JUMP at the kite.

But it's the sandwich he wants

... and he gets it too.

For a tiny dog he can jump a very long way.

Marcus forgets about the kite and runs after his dog.

He's really **strong** and **nippy**

(the dog – not Marcus).

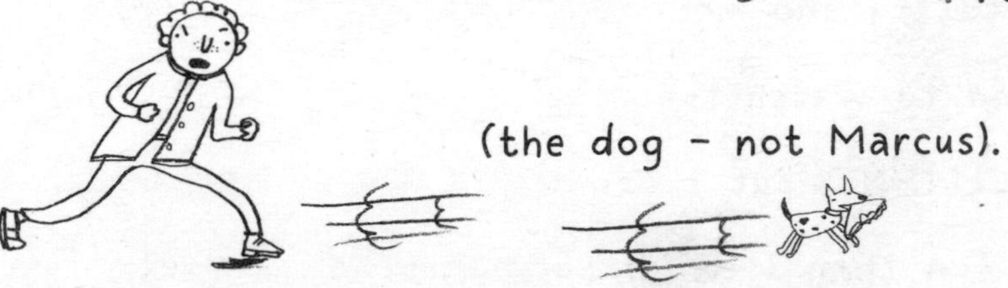

LUCKILY Marcus is out of sight when the wind drops and the kite sinks to the ground and lands with a CRASH.

Dad and I go and look at the broken kite.

"We can fix it," he tells me.

"At least it flew," I say.

Then we do a HIGH FIVE.

When we get home, Dad goes straight to the shed to try and mend the kite. And I'm FINALLY allowed to watch the rest of my CARTOON. Which is EXCELLENT. But I admit kite flying was a lot more fun than I expected. (I mustn't forget to take some string to school with me as well.)

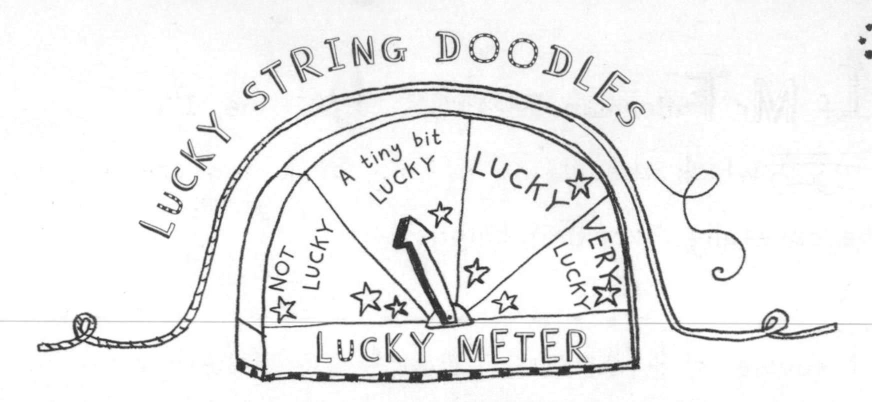

Having MY **EMERGENCY** string in these lessons is proving to be quite

.

It's keeping me occupied when Mr Fullerman's

starts sounding a bit like a robot and my mind starts wandering.

If Mr Fullerman **spots** me, I'll whisk the string off my desk and pretend to be carefully "working things out".

Trouble is, **Marcus keeps** STARING over in my direction. (Which isn't helping.)

He's going to get me into trouble if he doesn't

STOP BEING

NOSY!

"It's just a piece of string, Marcus," I tell him.

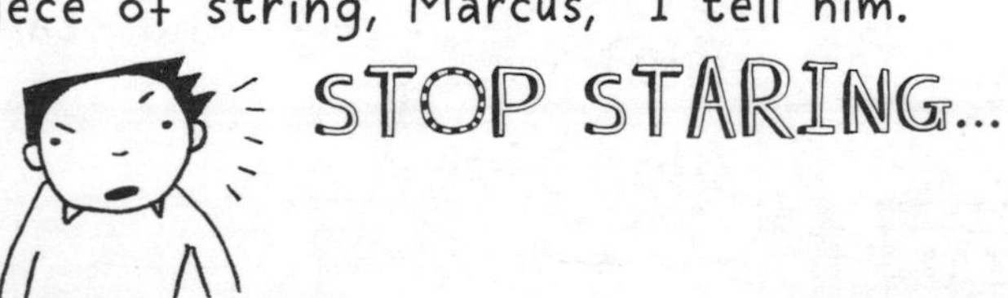

(Too late.)

"Thank you, Tom, I'll HAVE THAT!"
(Back to doodling, then.)

My lack of string means I'm down here on the Lucky Meter.

BACK AT HOME

This invitation arrived when I was in the front room doing my HOMEWORK (well, I was thinking about doing my homework).

WELCOME TEA PARTY

Hello, we're your new neighbours!
Rick, Sarah, our daughter June
and Roger the cat.

We're having a TEA PARTY!

You're all invited to come. We'd love to meet as many new FRIENDLY faces as possible!
From: 4 p.m. until 6.30 p.m.

I heard something being *SHOVED* through the letter box, so I went to see what it was. I took the envelope and RAN back into the front room so I could SNEAK a look out of the window and see who'd posted it. I got a **SHOCK** when I saw JUNE staring back at me. So I hid on the floor until she left. I looked at the envelope and thought it might be a letter complaining about me playing DUDE 3 too loudly again.

Boo!

It was addressed to:

EVERYONE at
24 Castle Road

So I opened it.

☺ Luckily it

wasn't bad news,

just the *TEA PARTY* invitation. I put it on the fridge like Mum does to make things

OFFICIAL.

WELCOME TEA PARTY
Hello, we're your new neighbours!
Rick, Sarah, our daughter June
and Roger the cat.

We're having a TEA PARTY!
You're all invited to come. We'd love to meet as
many new FRIENDLY faces as possible!
From: 4 p.m. until 6.30 p.m.

When Mum saw it she said, "That's nice – we can all get to know them a bit more."

(Which REALLY meant she could have a little **snoop** round their house. But I didn't say that.)

I called Derek just to check that he'd been invited too. I didn't want to be on my own at June's.

(He had. PHEW.)

That could have been awkward.

I'm about here right now I think.

On the day of the *TEA PARTY* Mum suddenly decided to make some biscuits. They SMELLED **delicious** when they were cooking but tasted absolutely

DISGUSTING.

Oh –

Yuck

"I must have mixed up the salt with the sugar," Mum said. Which is the sort of thing Granny Mavis does.

But the good news was Mum wanted me to go to the shop to "buy something nice QUICKLY!"

Add the sugar

SALT

sugar

(AS IF I'd pick something **horrible** to eat.) A **large** pack of CARAMEL wafers would be nice?

But the shopkeeper said they'd **sold out.**

I was SHOCKED at first, until luckily I spotted some delicious-looking

ICED DOUGHNUTS

in different COLOURS.

They lOOked VERY tasty. So I bought six doughnuts and some fruit chews with the change (for ME).

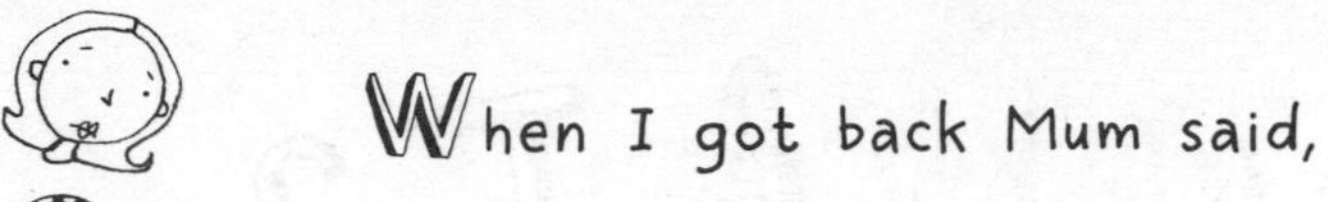

When I got back Mum said,

"OH dear, I hope they taste better than they look."

I thought they looked **YUMMY**. ☺

"They'll have to do," she added.

Dad came down wearing one of his slightly **ODD** T-shirts.

"Is THAT what you're wearing?" Mum asked him.

"It's **tea** with the NEIGHBOURS, not the QUEEN," Dad said, looking down at his T-shirt.

"Just don't eat too many cakes then," Mum said.

Dad and I wondered who she was talking to.

"Both of you – well, mostly you, Frank."

We are the first people to arrive at the neighbours' (which is awkward).

June's mum is wearing a long dress and her dad has a headband on. (Maybe my dad's T-shirt isn't so bad after all?)

They say hello to us and June's mum points to me and says, "You and June know each other already."

"We're in the same class," I say. And June says, "For now," like she knows something I don't. "Can I go and look for Roger? He's gone missing," she adds, ignoring me. June's mum nods, then asks if I'd like to go with her.

Not really - but I don't say that. Instead I say,

"No, thanks, I'm fine." But June's already gone.

"It's our cat, Roger. He keeps wandering off," her dad explains.

"He's probably in **our** house or digging up the plants in our garden!" I tell them. (Which is true.)

My mum gives me a nudge and June's parents look a bit embarrassed.

Mum changes the subject quickly and says, "We've brought something to add to the tea."

"That's very kind of you," June's mum smiles.

"You haven't seen what it is **yet!**" Dad says as a **JOKE**. (Mum doesn't laugh.)

"Do put it on the table next to my home-made cakes and bread," June's mum says. "I use all-natural ingredients and NO food colouring. So much nicer, don't you think?" she adds.

Mum's looking at the doughnuts I've just put on the table. "Yes, I suppose so – if you have the time."

(The doughnuts do stand out a LOT.)

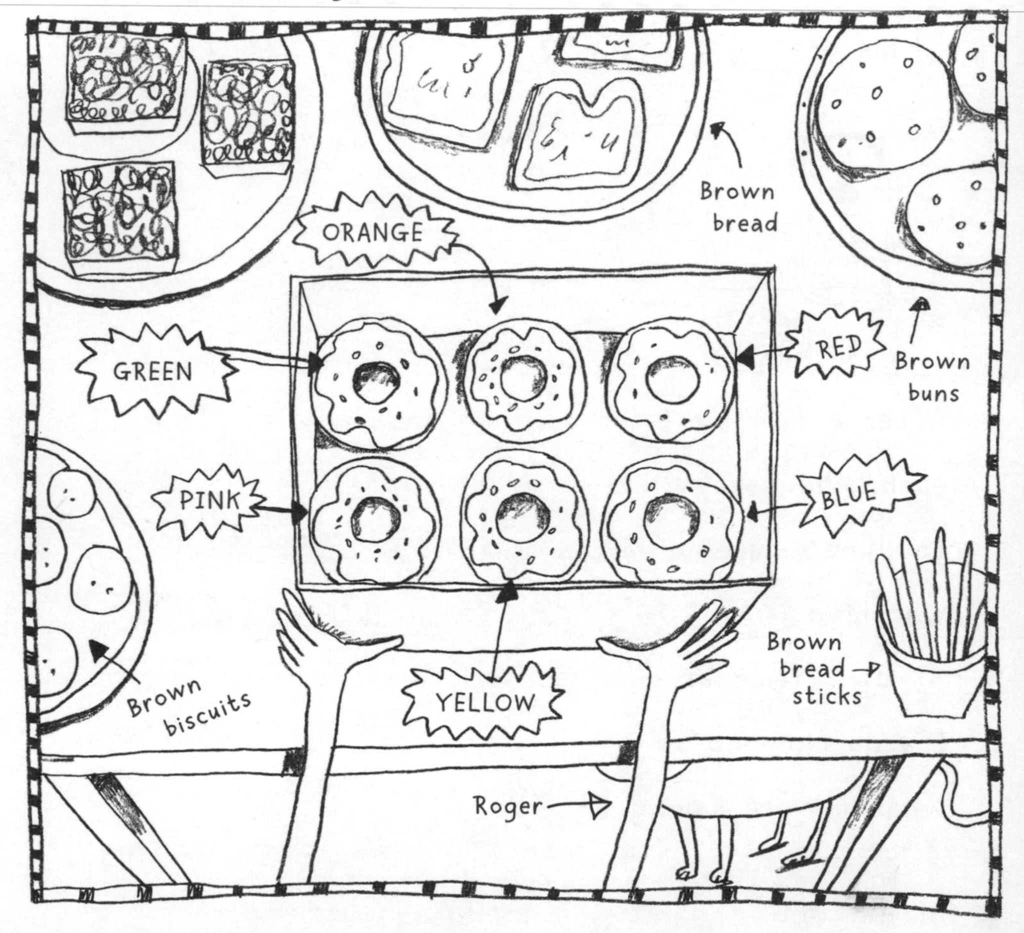

When Derek arrives, we go and TUCK into the "tea" before anyone else does. But we can't decide what to have *first*, so we take a bite out of a few different things first to see what's nice.

"This one's got BITS in it," Derek says, putting it back.

After a few more bites ... we choose a doughnut each. While we're eating I can hear my mum talking to June's parents about how much time I spend watching TV!

(Not as much as I'd LIKE to!)

I stop chewing so I can hear what they're saying BETTER.

June's mum says, "June doesn't watch TV because we don't have one."

Then for SOME REASON, my mum says,

If we got rid of our TV I wouldn't miss it at all.

Why's she saying THAT?

With a mouthful of doughnut I say really **LOUDLY**,

"I'D MISS THE TV. DON'T GET RID OF THE TV!"

Mum ignores me and carries on chatting like I haven't interrupted. Then she looks over and says,

And I'm thinking of ALL the TV programmes that I know Mum loves to watch. So in case she's forgotten, I keep reminding her of what she would MISS if we didn't have a TV.

Especially when she's talking to June's parents.

Derek says he has to go home to take Rooster for a walk.

(He's so lucky. I **wish** we had a dog.)

Now Derek's left, I'd like to go home as well. Mum's still chatting so I try and think of ways I can get Mum and Dad to go home.

I settle on telling Mum that I have LOADS of very important homework to do. "So I better go, if that's OK?"

"OK, Tom."

Dad says he'll come with me.

(I think he wants to leave as well.)

On the way out I NOTICE there's

One doughnut left. Seems a shame to leave it? It's not like I ate loads of other cakes or biscuits. Dad's just saying BYE when June's mum suddenly rushes past me, saying,

"SHOO, SHOO, get off the table, Roger!"

(Looks like June's cat's back then.)

Maybe I won't have that doughnut after all.

My comic

I **have** to do my homework now (I've got no choice) so I'm up in my room trying to get started. But I keep getting **good** ideas for a COMIC I'm making about some of the characters from

THE CRAZY FRUIT BUNCH.

Then I find this letter I must have shoved into my excercise book to keep safe. It's all about ENRICHMENT WEEK and what's going on in school. Next week we get to do different things in class than normal (which should be fun).

ENRICHMENT WEEK
at Oakfield School

Dear Parent/Carer,

hild will be taking part in Enrichment Week
ant topics: filmmaking,

The CRAZY FRUIT BUNCH

It was really funny when Norman Watson saw the letter. He asked, "Does EnRICHment Week mean we're all going to get RICH, sir?"

"No such luck, Norman,"

Mr Fullerman told him.

(Imagine if that really happened – how good would that be?)

Part of my homework is filling in my READING DIARY. The book I have is excellent (it's a DOCTOR PLANET book) – but I keep forgetting to get Mum or Dad to sign my diary so I've been signing it myself

with a squiggle.

NOW even if I remember, I can't get them to sign it, as they'll see what I've been up to.

I'm going to have to wait until the whole diary is filled up before I can get a new one.

Right, back to my homework ...

in a minute.

Here are two more **CRAZY FRUIT BUNCH** characters I made up.

As I'm drawing, I look into June's garden and can see her wander around searching for her cat again. She'll never find him there, because he's hiding in our garden. I could tap on my window and point out where he is? Or ...

... I could keep quiet. (Shhhhh.)

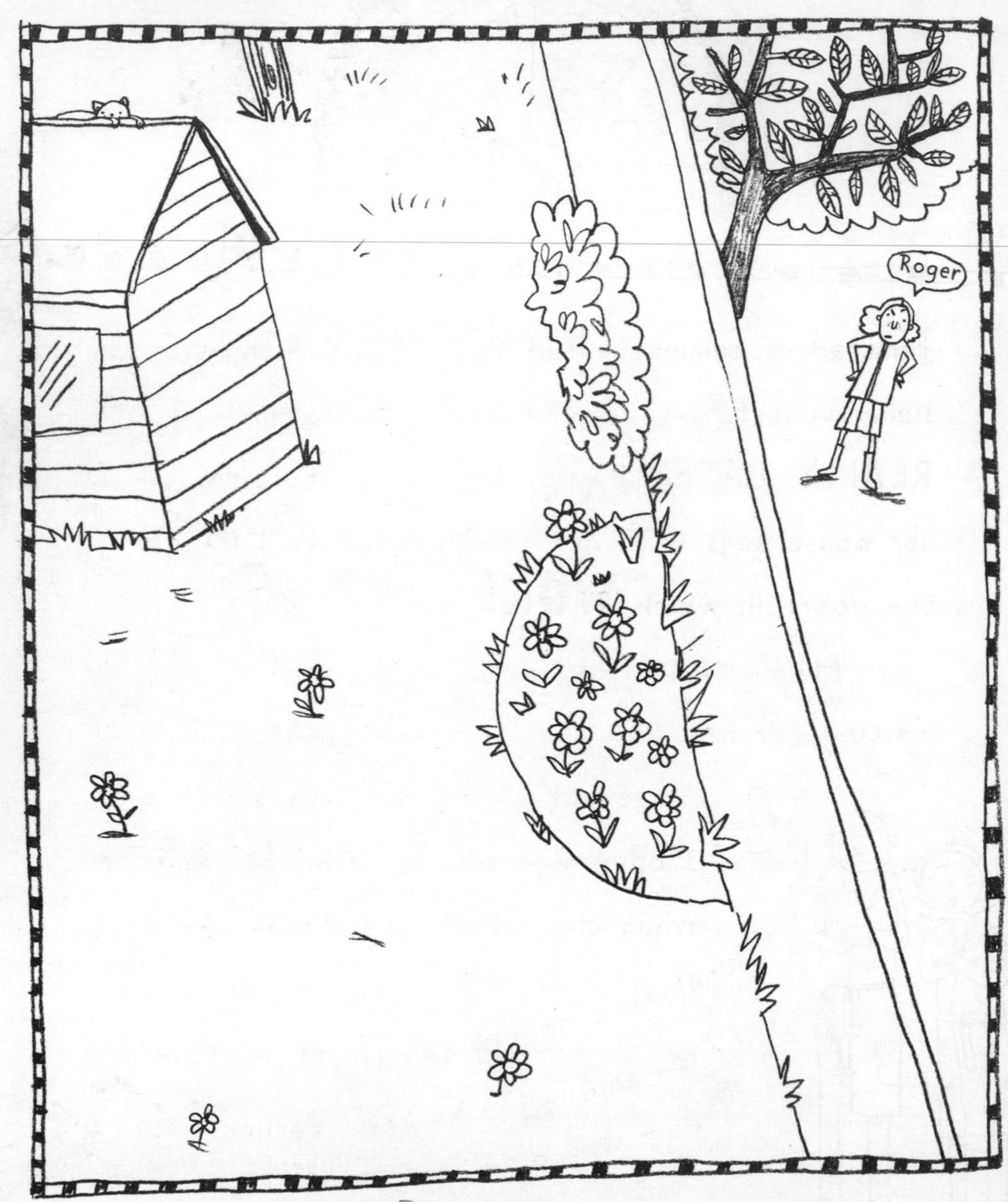

(Spot Roger the cat.)

Instead of coming to the TEA PARTY with us today, Delia went to meet her friends and came home REALLY LATE. She forgot to take her house keys with her too and had to ring the doorbell, which **WOKE** me up.

Mum and Dad are downstairs waiting for her. And they're not very HAPPY.

I get out of bed to have a listen. I open my door so I can HEAR what they are saying. Stuff like:

"What time do you call this?" and "You said you'd be home earlier – why didn't you call?"

I poke my head around the door to get a better listen,  but I can't quite hear what Delia is saying back to them...

Then a DOOR SLAMS and someone STOMPS up the stairs.

I QUICKLY JUMP back into bed...

as Delia goes past my room, then SLAMS her bedroom door as well. If I wasn't awake before – I definitely would be now.

Mum and Dad will probably have one of their little "CHATS" with her in the morning.

We're just disappointed

My guess is she'll be grounded for maybe a week? The only trouble with Delia being grounded is she mooches around the house the whole time, being even GRUMPIER than usual. If that's possible (which it is).

Mum and Dad are turning the lights off downstairs and coming to bed now. They're talking very quietly because they don't want Delia (or me) to hear what they're saying.

Which makes me listen EVEN harder.

I sneak out of bed again, but it's tricky to see in the dark and I accidentally TRIP over my SCHOOL SHOES. The ones I've thrown on the floor (along with a few other things). WHOOPS!

I manage to stop myself falling forward by GRABBING the side of a chair.

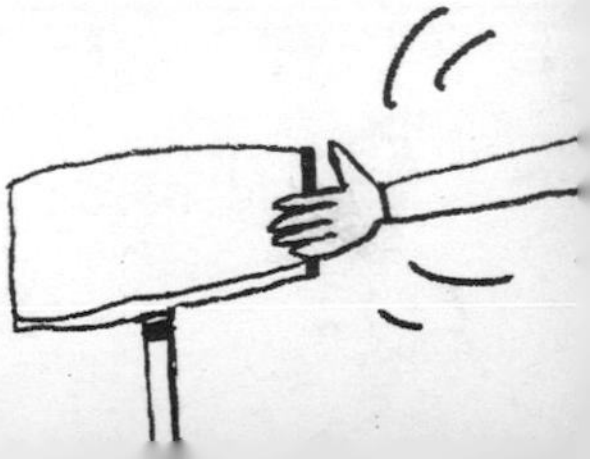

It knocks over a cup of hot chocolate with a nasty **THICK** milk skin on it (that I left because it looked disgusting). Uh oh!

Mum and Dad come running into my room. "What's going ON?" they both say, looking around at the mess. So I say, "The LOUD voices and doors slamming woke me up, and I couldn't see where I was going." Then I pick up my teddy and give it a little cuddle in case Mum and Dad get a bit cross about the stain on the floor. (Whoops.) I do my confused sleepy face too:

Dad gets a cloth to wipe up the chocolate. (Phew ... looks like I'm not in trouble.) "I'm a bit tired now," I tell them both. And Mum says she'll tuck me into bed (which is nice).

Then I say, I'm a bit thirsty as well.

So Mum gets me a drink of water.

I take a few sips, then put it to one side.

{{ SIGH... }}

Mum and Dad are smiling at me - so I probably shouldn't say...

I'm feeling a little hungry,
a caramel wafer might help?

"Nice try, Tom - goodnight."

(Oh well ...

if you don't ask...)

In the morning, there's no sign of Delia YET, as she's still in her room being all grumpy. I sit quietly at the kitchen table with my exercise book open, so it looks like I'm doing my homework. But I'm doodling instead.

When I turn the page, there's another letter that Mr Fullerman gave us about ENRICHMENT WEEK.

This one is supposed to REMIND us we're making pizzas and to bring in the ingredients for our toppings.

We don't usually do any cooking in our school, but with ENRICHMENT WEEK we get to try out NEW things. If it was up to me I'd add a few EXTRA things to the list to "TRY".

LIKE:

Caramel Wafer Juggling

AND

DOODLING

(with and without string).

That would be good!

We're not making REAL pizzas, we're just doing the toppings, so nothing too tricky (I hope).

Mr Fullerman gave us a piece of paper in class with a blank circle on it. We had to write down the ingredients, then draw what our pizza would look like.

Some kids thought it was more fun to make up really CRAZY pizza toppings and draw them. (Which was a mistake!)

Mr Fullerman picked up Brad's picture and read it out to everyone.

Chocolate, marshmallows and fish fingers. That's VERY interesting,

he said, and then sniffed in a slightly cross way.

ENRICHMENT WEEK Name: Tom Gates

What's going to be on YOUR pizza?
Write your name at the top, then ingredients here.
And draw a picture of what your pizza will look like.

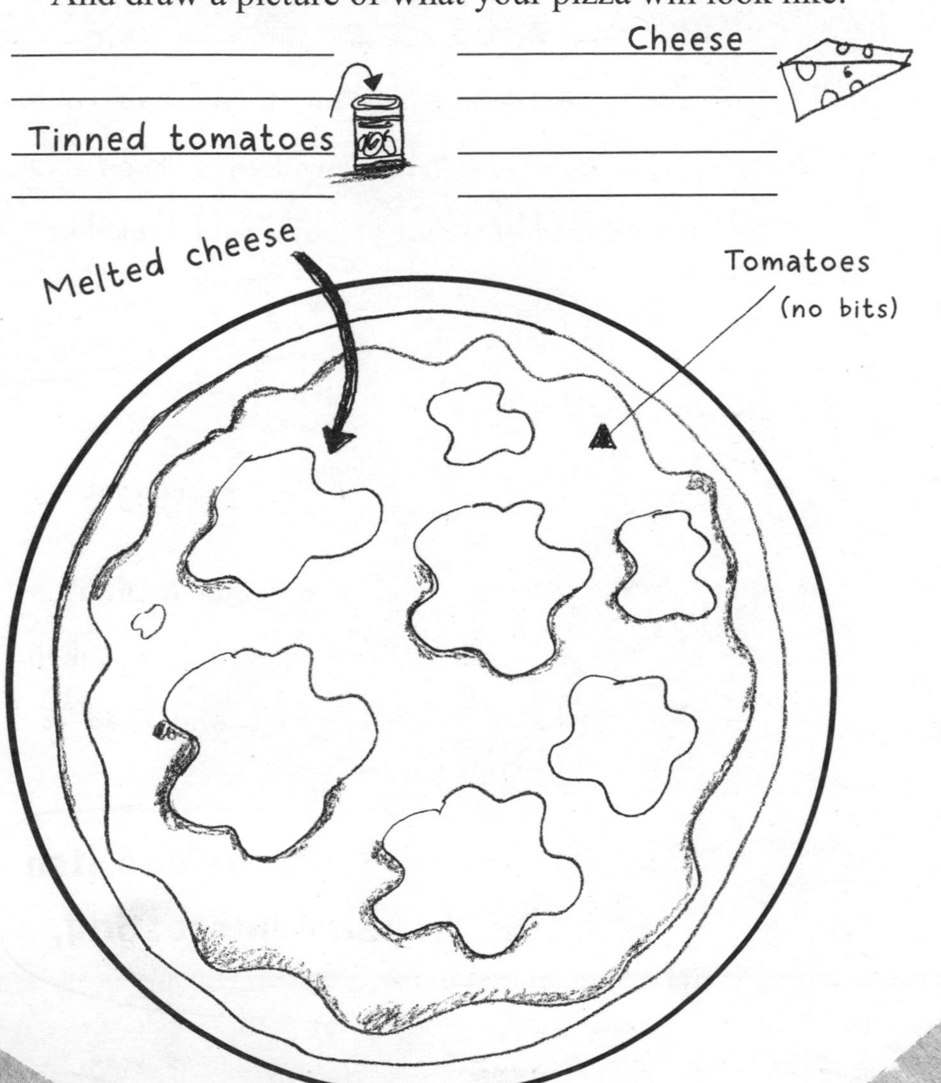

Brad was GIGGLING and smiling when Mr Fullerman added,

"Are you SURE that's what you want on your pizza, Brad?"

"I like to mix my flavours, sir."

(Which made us all laugh.) Ha! Ha! Ha!

I whispered to AMY,

"My Granny Mavis makes pizzas like that."

(It's true, she does.)

Then Mr Fullerman spotted Mark Clump's pizza list and read that aloud too.

"Raspberry jam, chips and cheese."

(Which made Julia Morton say, Eeww!)

REMEMBER, CLASS 5F. WHATEVER YOU PUT ON YOUR PIZZA, THAT'S WHAT YOU'LL BE EATING FOR YOUR LUNCH. I hope you like raspberry jam and chips, Brad and Mark!

They both put their hands up and asked for new pieces of paper.

My pizza was nice and easy (just two toppings). But I might bring a "backup snack" in case something goes wrong.

BURNT

(You never know.)

I carry on doodling and making up my own characters ...

... like THIS when FINALLY Delia appears. She looks extra gloomy too.

(Oh great.)

Mum and Dad hear she's up and come into the kitchen. They're trying to be all CHEERY and lighten the "mood" after telling her off last night. Which is a waste of time if you ask me.

Mum says, "We know you're cross with us, Delia."

(You can say that again.)

"But next time we agree a time for you to come home – just stick to it, will you?"

"I'm supposed to meet up with my friends to STUDY today. It's your fault if I get bad marks," Delia tells them.

(That's a good one – I'll have to remember that.)

"They can come HERE to study – you're just not allowed OUT with them for a WEEK."

A WEEK!

"Like I said ... if you need to study, invite them here."

Really? Dad doesn't look so sure.

"What's wrong with my friends?"

Delia wants to know.

I could tell her a few things. They all look like her, for a start.

Grumpy

Bit miserable

Stooped

Mum says that her friends can come over as long they don't:

- Play LOUD music
- Eat everything in the fridge
- Leave cups everywhere and generally make a mess.

"Then they're VERY WELCOME, Delia."

It's a TERRIBLE idea. It's bad enough having Delia sloping around the house without her friends here as well.

I'm hoping my **GOOD** behaviour and me leaving my exercise book open (to look like I'm working) is being noticed by Mum and Dad, so I can ask if Derek can come round too.

"Of course he can," Mum says.

"Don't go in my room," Delia groans.

But she always says that. It's not like I go in her room ALL the time. Well, only if I want to borrow something like:

- A **ROCK WEEKLY** magazine
- or a pen
- or maybe some music

and very occasionally a pair of black socks. And if she's been really annoying – I might borrow a pair of black sunglasses ...

... and HIDE them.

So not that often.

"Don't bug any of my friends either. I don't want you or Derek asking them stupid questions like 'What bands do you like?'"

Delia puts on a really SILLY VOICE which I think is supposed to be me.

"I don't speak like that," I tell her. The thought hadn't even crossed my mind to BUG Delia or her friends.

But NOW she's mentioned it – it might be fun. Ha! Ha!

Mum sighs. "Just be nice to each other, will you?" I carry on drawing and nod.

"Is that your homework?" Mum asks.

I could say YES, but it might be tricky to explain what subject it's for.

It's VERY important DOODLE homework.

So I tell her I'm just drawing and making up my own characters.

"They're really good, Tom," Mum says. "Oh, that reminds me..." And she gets out a

PUPPIES AND KITTENS calendar.

"A nice lady at my work thought you might like it because I told her you love dogs and drawings."

PUPPIES and KITTENS

"I wish we could get a REAL dog," I sigh.

"Well, bad luck – you can't. I'm ALLERGIC to dogs and cats," Delia reminds me.

Then she looks at the calendar and says,

"Why would ANYONE want something like that on their wall?" So I tell her, "Not everyone's ALLERGIC to cats and dogs, you know. I like it." (And because I am a NICE son I say "Thanks, Mum" and start looking at the pictures.)

"That's SO sweet!" Mum says when I show her a dog.

Dad is smiling at the cute puppies as well.

"Awww, look, that one's got a hat like mine!"

Delia's not impressed. "I can't listen to this, it's PATHETIC," she mutters before leaving.

While we carry on looking at the whole calendar.

Later that afternoon Derek comes over at **EXACTLY** the same time as Delia's friends arrive. Normally she'd take them straight upstairs to her room to work.

But today for SOME reason she's decided to bring all of them into the comfy front room. Which is VERY annoying because me and Derek have just sat down (to watch TV).

(The "please" bit is unusual.)

So I say, "Sorry, we were here first."

"Tom, we all need to sit here. Can you **move**?"

(I ignore her and Derek does the same.)

She's being all BOSSY and BIG SISTERISH with me in front of her friends.

(I ignore her and Derek does the same.)

"We could go to your room and try writing some more songs for our BAND BATTLE audition coming up?" Derek whispers to me.

I whisper back, "Yes, we *could* do that ...

And ANNOY Delia

(which is an EXTRA bonus).

As we're not budging, Delia's friends start chatting between themselves, which makes for a good listen.

"Did you hear that?" I *NUDGE* Derek and say.

"What other bands are entering then?" I ask Delia's friends. (Even though she told me NOT to talk to them.)

Dad **POPS** his head round the door and asks, "Everyone OK here?"

I'm about to say NO when Delia gets in FIRST.

"These two won't move - can you tell them to GO?"

"But we were here before them."

"Come on, Tom, Delia and her friends have work to do. Can you hang out somewhere else until they've finished?"

(Work? I'll believe THAT when I see it.)

Delia and her friends waft a book, a few bits of paper and a pen around. (Which is still not that convincing.)

But when Dad says,

How about how you go and get some fresh air?

I say, "OK, Dad, we'll go."

I tell Derek, "Let's think about what song to play at the BAND BATTLE audition."

Great idea, Tom, Dad says and he leaves us to it. Delia's friends are still chatting about the auditions so we take our time leaving. Which annoys Delia a bit more.

I heard that NERDY group who wear jumpers are auditioning too.

(No ... really?)

Then I make a **joke** and say,

They could put on their FLUFFY jumpers and call themselves NERD3!

NERD3

Derek and all Delia's friends start laughing.

(Delia doesn't.)

"If you're in a band, why would you even think of wearing a FLUFFY jumper on stage?" her friend wonders.

Then Delia decides to try and **EMBARRASS** me in front of everyone by telling them, "My little brother has a FLUFFY YELLOW KITTEN ONESIE – don't you, Tom? You could wear that in your band."

(Very funny, Delia.)

I tell her, "DOGZOMBIES are auditioning for BAND BATTLE and I'm NOT wearing a FLUFFY yellow kitten onesie because I DON'T have one – so THERE."

Then Derek whispers something in my ear.

"OK – I DID have a fluffy yellow kitten onesie* ... but I don't have it any more."

(Thanks for bringing that up, Delia.)

Delia starts shooshing me away with her hands.

Shoo

shoo

"Are you still here?" she asks.

I'm trying to think of something to say back to her, but my mind's gone blank.

*See *Best Book Day Ever* for the full yellow kitten onesie story.

"Why are you still here?" Delia says again.

"Errr, because I live here and he's my **mate**."

(Which is true and a good reply I think.)

"I'm sorry about these two – they're leaving now," Delia tells her friends.

(I've just thought of something ELSE to say.)

In a really loud voice, I tell them,

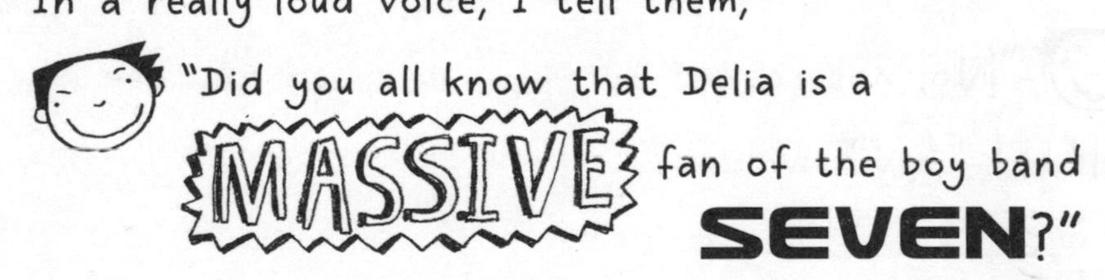

"Did you all know that Delia is a MASSIVE fan of the boy band **SEVEN**?"

"Ignore him – it's NOT TRUE and you're not funny, Tom."

(I am quite funny, because her friends are laughing and so is Derek.)

Ha! Ha! Ha! Ha!

I manage to get out of the way before

Delia lobs a cushion at us.

Derek's still LAUGHING and says, "Your sister was CROSS about that, wasn't she? Does she really like **SEVEN**?"

"No, not really." But I've just had another BRILLIANT idea.

While Delia is doing her "college work" Derek and I find lots of pictures of **SEVEN** ...

SEVEN
Good work
SEVEN
SEVEN
SEVEN
... and decorate
her bedroom with them.

SEVEN
SEVEN
SEVEN
SEVEN
SEVEN
SEVEN

Luckily for Derek, he's gone home by the time Delia brings her friends up to her room. From the way she's

SHOUTING my name – TOM!

I'm guessing she's not that keen on the new posters? I keep my door closed until she calms down.

(Which takes a while.)

Mum and Dad make me take the pictures down and apologize to her. (It was still worth it, though.) I keep out of Delia's way and do a few drawings from the **PUPPIES AND KITTENS calendar** Mum gave me. And in my exercise book I find the OFFICIAL letter about ENRICHMENT WEEK.

Which I should have put it on the fridge. I draw a few cats and dog on it instead. It's not like I'll FORGET what I'm doing or anything.

Cat kite

ENRICHMENT WEEK
SCHOOL INSPECTION

Dear Parents/Carers,

This week we will be having a SCHOOL INSPECTION AND ENRICHMENT WEEK.

This is a chance for the children try out new activities. School lessons will continue in some subjects as normal.

Your form teachers will have shown your child a list of the activities, including any EXTRA items they might need to bring into school.

It's going to be a FANTASTIC experience for them all.

Please can children be ON time and have the CORRECT uniform on too.

Thank you,

Mr Keen

Headmaster

(The letter looks more fun now.)

June has already left for school ... and is walking ahead of me and Derek. We're TOO busy laughing about how we REDECORATED Delia's room to catch up.

Ha! Ha!

We're nearly at school when Derek says, "I think we're making a short film this week."

"What, with the whole class?" I wonder.

"Yes, even Mrs Worthington is going to be in it," Derek tells me.

And I say,

Which makes Derek laugh.

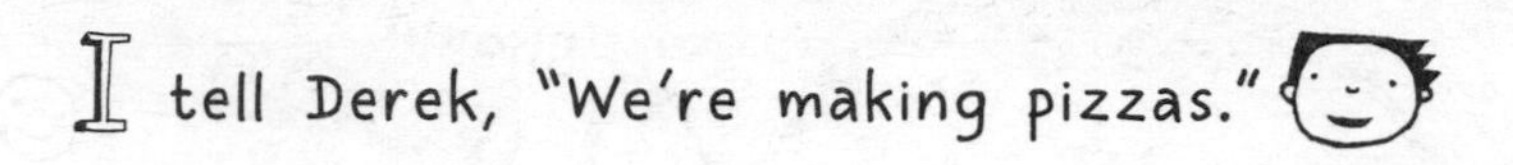

I tell Derek, "We're making pizzas."

AS SOON AS I SAY THE WORD

PIZZAS I SUDDENLY REMEMBER

I'VE LEFT MY PIZZA TOPPINGS

AT HOME!

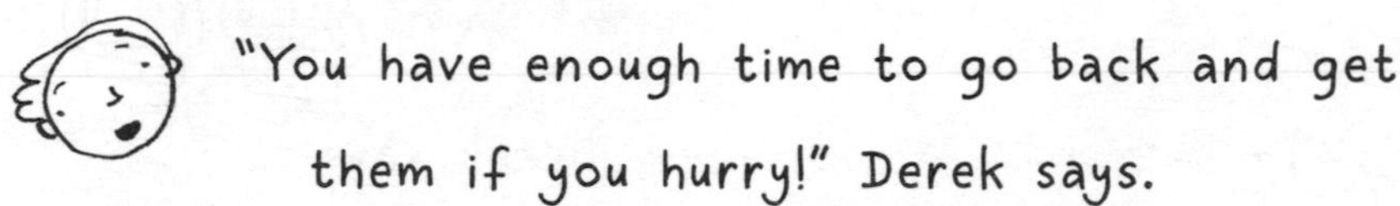

"You have enough time to go back and get them if you hurry!" Derek says.

So that's what I do. I RUN back home. (Luckily I don't live far away.)

I open the front door and *CHARGE* into the kitchen, saying,

"MUM ... cheese ... tomatoes ... Mum ... please CHEESE!"

Mum's already gone to work and it looks like Dad's out too. Or he's in the shed and can't hear me.

So I LOOK in the fridge first.

Cheeses, cheese...
What cheese...

THERE'S CHEESE EVERYWHERE. Which one do I choose? Just in case, I take ALL of them and shove everything in my bag.

Then I go to the cupboard to find a tin of

and TWO things happen when I open the door:

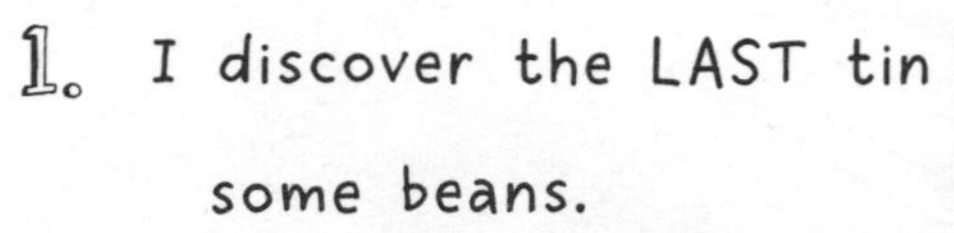

1. I discover the LAST tin

hidden behind some beans.

2. As I grab it – I knock over a BAG of flour.

BAD ☹

then **LANDS** on the floor ... and all the flour ...

(And I mean EVERYWHERE!)

It's a MESS.

I try scraping the flour back in the bag with my hands. Which sort of works – until I drop it again. The flour PUFFS up and goes in my face. There's not enough time to clear up or I'll be late for school.

So I shove the bag back in the cupboard and

accidentally tread in a pile of flour

at the same time

(I forgot my shoes have HOLES in them).

Pushing the flour into the corner of the kitchen

makes it look a tiny bit better.

(There, all done.)

Now I grab my bag and head to the

door, leaving flour footprints as I go.

As I'm walking to school the flour starts

puffing out of the holes in my shoes

and it begins to  RAIN too. Which

makes me a bit **SOGGY** because I've forgotten

my coat. (Great.)

When I FINALLY get to school ...

something's different?

The school entrance looks all CLEAN and TIDY. (Which is unusual.)

Mr Sprocket is at the door and HE looks VERY SMART.

(Not like me.)

"Just in time, Tom. What happened to you?" he asks me.

"I had an accident with a bag of flour, sir."

"You'd better go and clean up a bit, then," Mr Sprocket tells me.

"Yes, sir."

When I see myself in the mirror, I don't look THAT bad. I brush away some of the flour, then head OFF to class so I'm not late. Mr Fullerman looks very smart too. He's even wearing ...

"Hurry up and sit down, Tom, you're nearly LATE."

"Sorry, sir," I say as flour puffs out of my shoes. AMY PORTER looks at me.

"What happened to you?"

"Long story," I say.

(It's too embarrassing to explain what really happened, and I don't want June asking me questions too.) Then I notice ... she's not there. Her desk's gone as well.

"Where's June?" I ask AMY.

"She's moved to Mr Sprocket's class, because it's smaller and she has more friends there."

"No more listening to her saying 'DUDE3 are rubbish' for me then!" I say cheerfully.

Mr Fullerman announces,

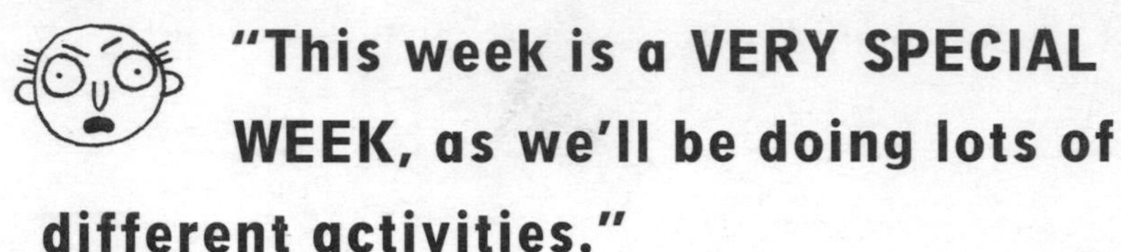

"This week is a VERY SPECIAL WEEK, as we'll be doing lots of different activities."

(Excellent!)

"And there will be uniform checks too."

(Mr Fullerman is STARING at me.)

"Now – has everyone remembered to bring their PIZZA TOPPING ingredients?"

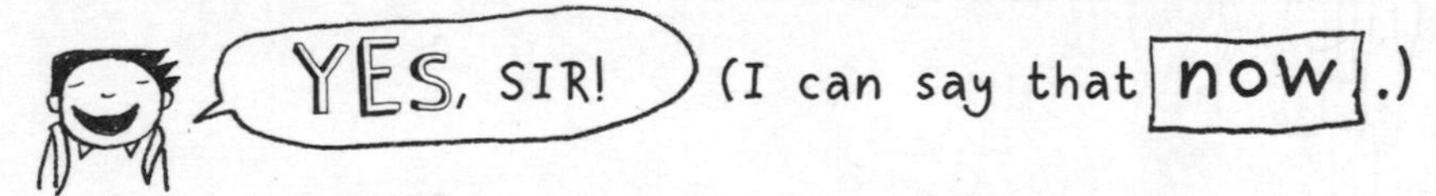

(I can say that now.)

The ingredients are in my bag. I take it off and put it on the back of my chair.

There's a WEIRD smell wafting around, but I can't tell where it's coming from. We have ASSEMBLY this morning, so Mr Fullerman says we'll be making the pizzas when we come back. (I can't wait!)

As my bag is a bit damp from the rain, I push the chair near a radiator to help it dry out a bit while I'm gone. (Good thinking.) When Class 5F get to the hall, Mr Keen is wearing a SUIT and TIE!

In fact, ALL the teachers are looking unusually smart. Solid (who's sitting behind me) says,

"The school's being inspected this week - that's why they're all looking so *FANCY.*"

(That makes sense.)

Mr Keen says, **"Morning, Oakfield School."**

"Morning, Mr Keen," we reply.

"You might notice that this week we have school inspectors here. So I'll be expecting correct school uniforms, no LATENESS and EXCELLENT BEHAVIOUR!" (Not much then.)

On the way back to class, Norman tries to get my attention by jumping

But one LOOK from Mr Fullerman

and he stops pretty quickly.

Solid tells me, "Teachers get a lot more STRICT when there's an inspection." And we've got a WHOLE WEEK of this too. (Great.)

Mr Fullerman makes us all line up outside the classroom.

Listen carefully, Class 5F. I want hard work and concentration – no chatting, messing around or doodling, OK?

THERE'S A TERRIBLE SMell!

All the kids go WILD and start making noises like ...

EEEEEEEwwwwwwwwwwwwww AGHHHHHHHH

OWWWWWWWWw

"What's that SMELL, sir?"

"I'm not sure, we might have to open a window."

Marcus is clutching his stomach and pretending to be sick.

"It's disgusting!"

It's not great and as I get closer to my chair I realize that the SMELL is coming from around ... my desk?

Even with the window open the smell is still really BAD so I sit down and open my bag.

AND THAT'S WHEN THE SMELL GETS EVEN

WORSE!

Marcus is pointing at ME and saying,

"It's Tom Gates, sir!"

WHAT?

"It's not ME, sir, it's my bag ... I think."

Mr Fullerman is telling everyone to

"SIT DOWN AND BE QUIET, PLEASE!"

at exactly the same time as a SCHOOL INSPECTOR appears with his clipboard.

From the look on his face I think he's just got a WHIFF of the smell too.

Mr Fullerman peers into my bag and winces...

"I think your cheese is a bit RIPE, Tom."

"Ripe? Like a piece of fruit?" I wonder.

Mr Fullerman tips ALL my cheese out on to my desk. Which makes Marcus *LURCH* away and say, "EEEEEEEEWWWWWW."

(He's so annoying.)

"Did you want all this cheese on your pizza, Tom?"

"Not really, sir," I tell him while holding my nose.

"How much cheese did you bring?"

"I panicked, sir. I was in a hurry."

Mr Fullerman says, **"Don't worry, I'll deal with the cheese"** and takes it away.

Marcus keeps **COUGHING** and overreacting.

"Very funny, Marcus. The smell's gone now," I say. (Well ... nearly.)

AMY  says I can have a piece of her  cheese for my pizza, as mine is all gone now. Which is nice of her.

Thanks, Amy

By the time Mr Fullerman comes back, the pong is not as bad, so everyone starts to settles down a bit more, apart from  Marcus, who keeps holding his nose and saying,

"EEEEEEEEEWWWWWWW cheese," at me.

"You're hilarious, Marcus," I tell him.

(He's not.)

"Right, Class 5F," Mr Fullerman says.

"Let's make those PIZZAS, shall we?"

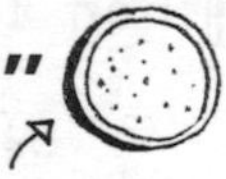

We've all been given plain ready-cooked pizza bases and a piece of special greaseproof paper to put them on. As we don't have ovens in the classroom, all the pizzas are being cooked in the school kitchen for our lunch.

"Has everyone washed their hands and put on an apron?"

Mr Fullerman checks.

We all say, "YES, SIR!"

Apart from Norman, who's already eaten half his cheese and can't speak with his mouth full. All I have to do is (carefully) open my tin of tomatoes with a tin opener and tip them into a bowl. Then I spread some tomato on the pizza base, which is easy enough (well, for some people).

Mess

Then I grate some cheese on top of the tomato ...

and it's all done.

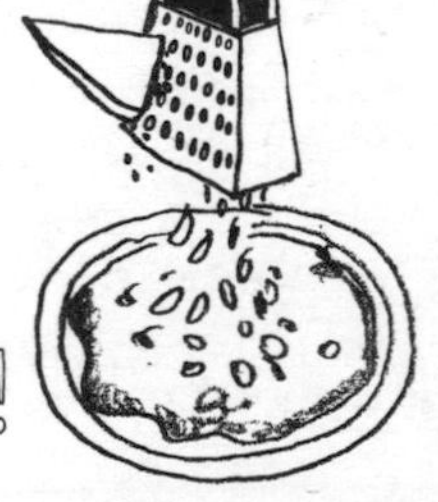

BRILLIANT!

My pizza is a masterpiece and ...

... doesn't look **anything** like the pizzas **Granny Mavis** sometimes makes.

When the school inspector was in our class I noticed he did a **LOT** of writing. Now he's gone I'm lOOking at all the PIZZAS everywhere and feeling a bit **peckish**. (It's a good JOB I have a "backup snack".)

I take out my pencil case, which has a secret compartment stuffed full of chocolate raisins, and open it up. I pick off the odd pencil shaving that's stuck to them.

As I'm quietly tipping the raisins on to the table, **AMY** asks me a question and makes me JUMP.

"Have you finished already, Tom?"

"Yes, mine's done," I say, showing her my handiwork. But when I turn back round to finish eating the rest of my raisins ...

they're all GONE?

"Where are my raisins?" I'm looking around and I suddenly SPOT them on top of Marcus's PIZZA. "What are you doing, Marcus?" I ask him.

"What does it look like I'm doing – I'm putting OLIVES on my pizza," he tells me crossly.

"Marcus - you know they're NOT olives, don't you?" I tell him.

"All I know is that MY pizza is going to be the BEST," he says smugly.

"But Marcus - they were MY..."

"Oh well ... too late, Tom," he says. "They're on my pizza now."

(It's not like I didn't TRY to tell him.) 

Mr Fullerman gets everyone's attention and says,

"So you know whose pizza belongs to who, write your names on the greaseproof paper. And well done, Class 5F – they all look delicious."

(Some pizzas are more delicious than others...)

I write my name really clearly because I know whose pizza I don't want to eat.

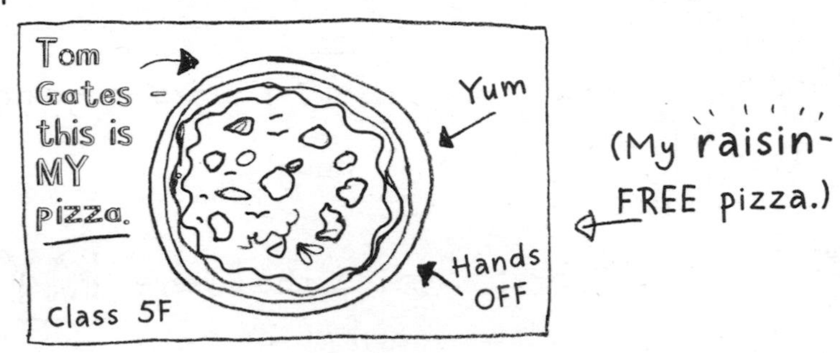

When the bell goes for the break I find Derek so I can tell him about:

1. My cheese-Smell disaster. (Shame.)

2. What song we should play for the BAND BATTLE AUDITION - we have to decide soon.

Marcus walks past and says, "EEEEEEEEWWWWWWW cheese" at me AGAIN. Which is annoying.

EEEEEEWwww cheese

We try and ignore Marcus when Norman comes over and starts sniffing the air.

He's right – there **is** a nice smell of cooking wafting from the school kitchens. We follow the smell and all PEER through the windows looking for our pizzas.

Nope, I can't see anything. But the smell is making me hungry.

Derek says, "I wish I was making a pizza."

"My pizza is going to be **DELICIOUS**," Marcus announces.

"Maybe?" I say (while thinking, Maybe **not**).

Burnt raisi

I tell Derek he can have some of my pizza.

Then I have **an** idea for the film his class is making. "How about ... the school inspectors are really aliens in disguise? And they want to take **over** the school first ...

... **then** the world!"

"Good idea," Derek says.

So I carry on...

"If you're late for class they ZAP you when you're least expecting it."

ZAP

(I do some zapping noises.)

"I think that school inspector in our class **could** be an ALIEN." (Now I do an alien impression. Which makes everyone laugh.)

Ha! Ha!

"I am an **alien school inspector**.

I am an **alien school inspector**."

So I do it again.

"I am an **alien school inspector**. I AM–"

I don't get to finish what I'm saying because the school inspector finishes it for me...

(Oops? Unlucky...)

LATE FOR CLASS?
Off you go. Quickly.

Great - now I'm looking over my shoulder all the time in case a school inspector is *lurking* behind me. (Groan.)

I'm walking back to class (quickly) when I see that AMY and Florence have noticed the nice cooking smells too.

"I hope that's our pizzas!" I say to them.

AMY asks me, "Why aren't you in the music room practising?"

"What for?"

"Aren't you auditioning for BAND BATTLE?"

"Yes - but we've got loads of time to practice," I tell them.

Florence says, "There's a group of kids from Year Six who've already got an audition - and they're practising like crazy."

"Really?"

"Mr Sprocket said it was OK." 

 "Did he?"

"I've heard they're REALLY GOOD!" 

"So are DOGZOMBIES. We'll be fine, we have an idea for the audition," I say confidently.

(It's sort of true.)

Then as we go into class Marcus walks past me and says,

AGAIN.

If he does that one more time, I'm going to tell him those raisins on his pizza are really small BUGS.

(I might do that anyway.)

After break, I go back to class, and Mr Fullerman is tapping his watch. **"Hurry up – we can't have the school inspector thinking you're late for class all the time, can we?"**

The GOOD NEWS is there are loads of interesting drawing things around. Excellent – this is my kind of lesson! We have to decorate and design our own placemats for our pizza lunches.

"You can make a group table decoration too – there's a special prize for the best and most creative one!" Mr Fullerman tells us. (I love a prize!)

Here's MY decorated mat, which I'm really happy with!
Yum
Hands OFF
My pizza goes here
TOM GATES

Now I've finished drawing on my placemat, I have a good think about what kind of table decoration I could make from this lump of clay. (I have a few ideas.) Marcus is drawing a picture of his own  face on his placemat.

He tells me, "I don't want anyone else eating my pizza. This will stop them."

Get Lost

MINE

No one's going to eat your pizza, Marcus.

(Especially with those chocolate raisins  on it.)

But I don't say that ... YET. Instead I start making a MONSTER out of the clay.

"That looks good, Tom," AMY says.  "Shall I make a stand for it?" Which is a good idea because it's a bit wobbly.

Marcus sees what we're doing and reminds us, "It's supposed to be a GROUP table decoration. What shall I do?"

I sigh ...

... then I suggest Marcus draws another picture of HIMSELF. "With legs – not just your HEAD this time, and make it THIS **BIG** so I can cut it out. Can you do that?"

"**Duh.** Of course I can, I'm not an idiot, you know."

(I say nothing.)

Marcus does a drawing and gives it to me. "What are you going to do with it?" he wants to know. I'm still making the monster, but I tell him,

"You'll see – it'll be good."

"It better be if we want to win the prize."

There ... all done.

Now Marcus is **COMPLAINING** about being eaten by my MONSTER.

"Why does it have to be me?"

"It looks really good, though, doesn't it, Marcus?"

"I'm going to do a NEW drawing of YOU, Tom," he tells me. Then Mr Fullerman comes over and CONGRATULATES us on making a **"fantastic table decoration. Whose idea was it to put a drawing with the monster?"**

Before I can say anything, Marcus says, "It was mine, sir, and my drawing too."

(Typical ... even AMY is rolling her eyes.)

"I thought you wanted to change it, Marcus?" I remind him.

"Not now."

While Marcus is still being ALL SMUG, I pop a bit of chalk into my pocket for our next breaktime. (Chalk is useful for drawing on the ground, which might come in handy.) SMUG

As we've finished doing everything a lot earlier than Mr Fullerman expected, he REMINDS us about our READING DIARIES. **"I hope you are keeping your reading diaries up to date, Class 5F?"**

I say, Yes, sir, even though I haven't. Then Mr Fullerman says he'll read us a story for a change. **"Would you like that?"** he asks.

There's a big chorus of YES, SIR, with Norman jumping up and down out of his seat. We all quieten down and listen.

Mr Fullerman holds up the book he wants to read, which looks interesting. He's good at doing all the diferent voices too.

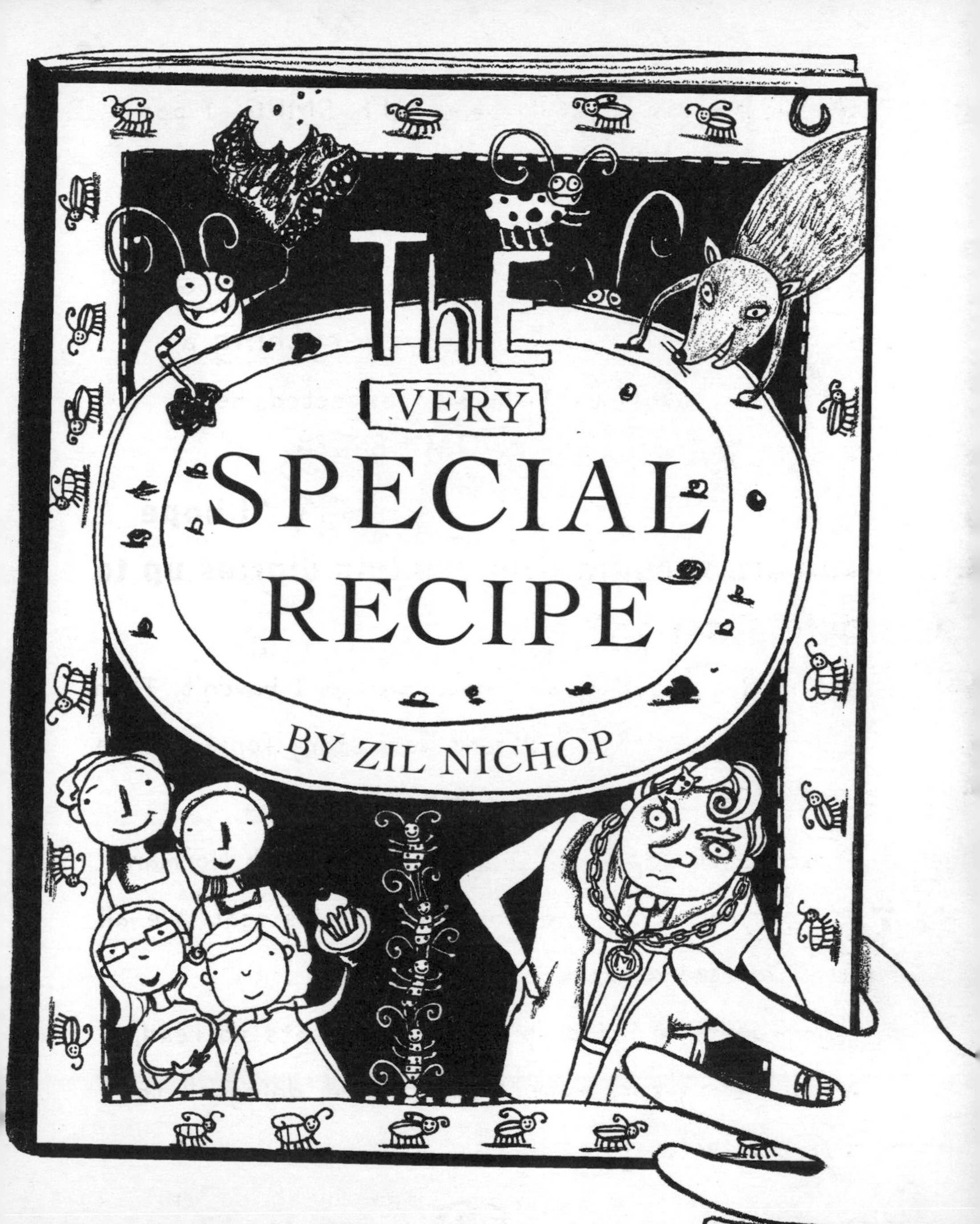
ThE
VERY
SPECIAL
RECIPE
BY ZIL NICHOP

WARNING:

THIS STORY CONTAINS:

BUGS

COCKROACHES

RATS

MICE

BAD HAIR

BAD PEOPLE WITH BAD HAIR

BAD HAIR THAT'S REALLY A SQUIRREL.

(BUT NOT NECESSARILY IN THAT ORDER.)

...AND A LOT OF OTHER

ODD THINGS AS WELL.

So if you're feeling a little bit queasy or have a slightly weak stomach, may I suggest that you put this book down RIGHT now and go and find something else to read instead . . .

. . . or take up knitting (or do both).

Because some of this story might have you reaching for a BUCKET. And I'm not even going to HINT at how the story ends, as just THINKING about it makes me feel ill.

STILL HERE?

Well, don't say I didn't warn you about the gross stuff.

LOOK!

There's one of those disgusting bugs now.

(I told you they were horrid.)

Dribble

CHAPTER ONE

In the dead of night, one tiny little cockroach scuttled along a pipe and headed towards the delicious smell of food that was wafting towards him. If cockroaches could TALK, this one would have been calling out over his shoulder, *"Hey, come on, everyone, follow me THIS WAY!"* (But as far as I know, cockroaches can't talk, so you'll just have to use your imagination here.)

Hundreds more cockroaches poured through the pipe behind him. The closer they got to the light and the smell from THE TEA SHOP, the more their legs picked up speed.

The bugs spilled through the open grate and hit the ground like a cockroach

STARBURST,

scattering in every direction ready to EXPLORE their new home. Across the shelves, up the walls and over tables they ran. This was about to become the **biggest** COCKROACH TEA PARTY EVER.

"Wooo hoooo, what a GREAT place!"

"We've struck LUCKY HERE!"

the cockroaches were saying (or WOULD be saying – if they could talk).

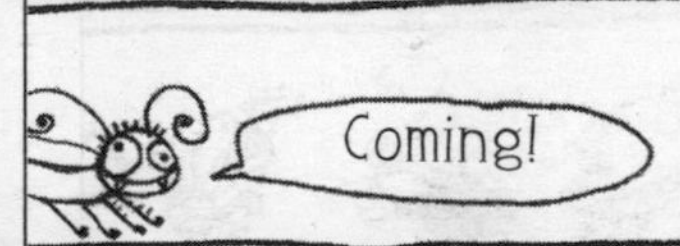

THE TEA SHOP was packed full of freshly baked cakes, biscuits, bread, rolls, iced buns and chocolate éclairs. There were stacks of macaroons, brownies and flapjacks all piled up high in the glass display counters. The sliding doors were firmly closed (for now). The thick layer of bugs scratched and desperately searched for a way to get inside.

But when the rats and the mice arrived, they knew exactly what to do next. A push here, a slide there, and the glass doors were open. The bugs quickly smothered the tasty treats and began to chomp and BITE their way through everything. The whole TEA SHOP was teeming with creatures excitedly chewing and crunching. They didn't stop eating until the sun came up, and there wasn't a SINGLE treat left that hadn't been nibbled, tasted, squashed, trodden in – or much worse.

And if cockroaches could talk, they would be saying, *"I'm SO full I couldn't eat another crumb."* Or *"GREAT tea party, wasn't it?"* But like I said, they can't, so just keep using your imagination.

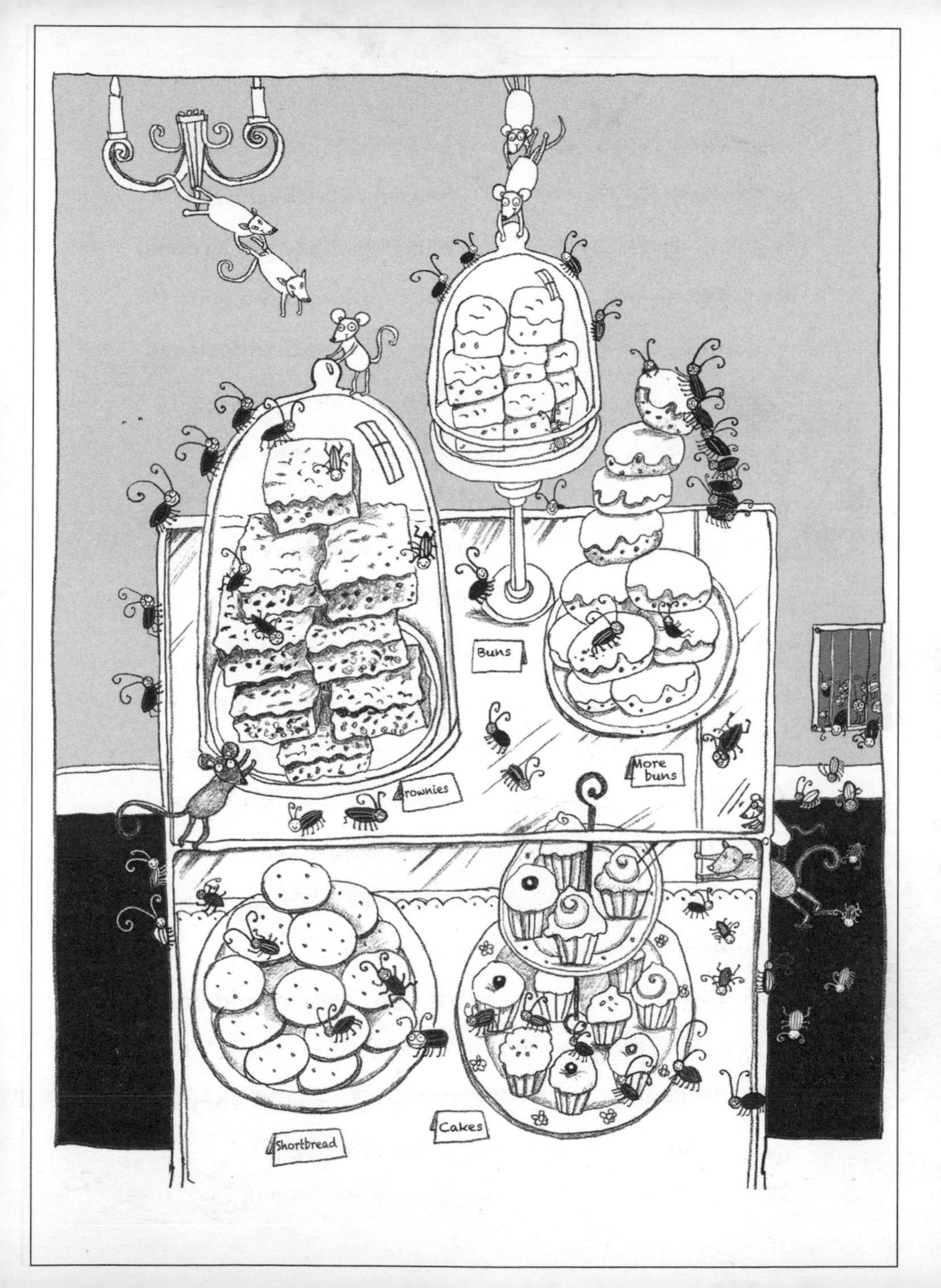

Buns
More buns
Brownies
Cakes
Shortbread

When Apple and Plum Crumble decided to go downstairs EARLY (for a change), the last thing that either of them expected to see when they opened the door was ...

THE TEA SHOP was in a terrible state. It was a DISASTER! They called out for their mum and dad to come quickly.

"LOOK WHAT'S HAPPENED!" they shouted.

The food inspectors and the mayor were due to arrive that afternoon.

"What are we going to do now?" Apple said, looking around at the chewed cakes.

"Mum and Dad will know what to do. Don't panic. They always think of something," Plum told her confidently.

(Exactly WHAT that "something" was . . .
you'll have to keep reading to find out.)

Mr Fullerman *SLAMS* the book closed and says, **"Right, who's ready for some lunch?"**

I wanted to hear more of the story!

AAAAAAwwwwwwwwwwwwwwwwwww

the class all say.

"We can read some more later. It's time for your tasty pizzas. You must all be hungry?"

(I know I am.)

Julia Morton puts her hand up and says, "Mr Fullerman – I'm not THAT hungry after the story."

Those bugs haven't put anyone else off their lunch, as there's a mad RUSH to be first in the dinner queue.

Mrs Mumble is trying to make sure that we all walk s l o w l y. Best behaviour, she tells us, mouthing the word INSPECTORS so we don't forget they're here. I was hoping to be much nearer the front of the queue. But somehow (despite some very fast walking) me, Solid and Norman are almost at the back. Which is ANNOYING when I'm so hungry. Even MORE ANNOYING is Marcus has managed to wheedle his way to the front.

How did he get there? Solid wonders.

I'm pretty sure I know how.

"Follow me," I say. We nip along a different staircase, which brings us to another door – and almost to the front of the queue. I wait for Mrs Mumble to get distracted. Then we all sneak in.

Mrs Mumble is busy showing one of the inspectors where to sit down. As he walks past I whisper to Solid, "He caught me doing an ALIEN impression of him." We all try our best to lOOk like we've been at the front of the queue the WHOLE time and haven't taken a short cut at all.

(innocent)

By the time Marcus realizes where we're standing, it's too late for him to **COMPLAIN**. huh?

Mrs Mumble says we can go in now. (Result!) I head straight to the table with our decoration on it.

My pizza is on my placemat along with everyone else's. It's a PIZZA FEAST!

And even better ... my pizza tastes delicious. Everything is going really well – right up until Marcus goes and makes that STUPID noise at me again.

EEEEEEEEWWWWWW cheese!

(OK, that does it.)

I take a really good look at his PIZZA, then say,

"Marcus, you know those aren't OLIVES on your pizza, don't you?"

And he says, "Yes they are – I put them on."

Then Pansy (who's sitting next to Marcus) leans over and says, "They don't look like olives to me. I don't know what they are." (I do.)

"What do they taste like then?" I ask Marcus. He pops a big piece into his mouth and says,

"They taste ...

... yummy! Mmm."

(He's pretending to like the BURNT chocolate raisins on his pizza.)

"Who'd have thought FLIES on a pizza would taste **that** good, Marcus?" I say.

"Very funny, Tom. I'm not falling for that trick," he says.

Pansy stares at them a bit more. "You're eating flies?"

"He doesn't believe me – but you can see their legs," I tell her.

Marcus is beginning to wonder if I might be right. He starts poking at one of the raisins, then picks it up with his fingers for a close inspection.

I say (just to make the point).

Marcus starts wafting the raisin under Pansy's nose...

"See, it's **not** a **FLY.**"

Which makes Pansy *LURCH* away from the suspected fly. Then Julia Morton hears the word "FLY" and turns round really *FAST*, so water spills all over the table from the jug she's holding. And the kid next to her accidentally drops his pizza on the floor.

Mrs Mumble hears someone shout AGH! and comes running over to see what's going on. "No shouting, please," she says STERNLY just before she slips on the slice of pizza and **SHOUTS** AGHH! really loudly ...

right across the floor. She stops herself from falling over by grabbing hold of the table. But she makes the whole table WObbLe so a plate of jelly and custard balanced on the edge tips over and lands right in the lap of guess who?

(Yes - THAT school inspector.) Who doesn't look very pleased.

I'm not the only kid laughing - but for some reason he looks right at ME - like it's my fault!

I stop straight away.

(Something else to write about me in the school report - groan.)

LUCKILY Caretaker Stan comes to the rescue and arrives just in time with his super-sized mop and cloth to help clean the mess up. I'm not sure how well this school inspection is going but my guess is we'd be about HERE on an inspection meter right now.

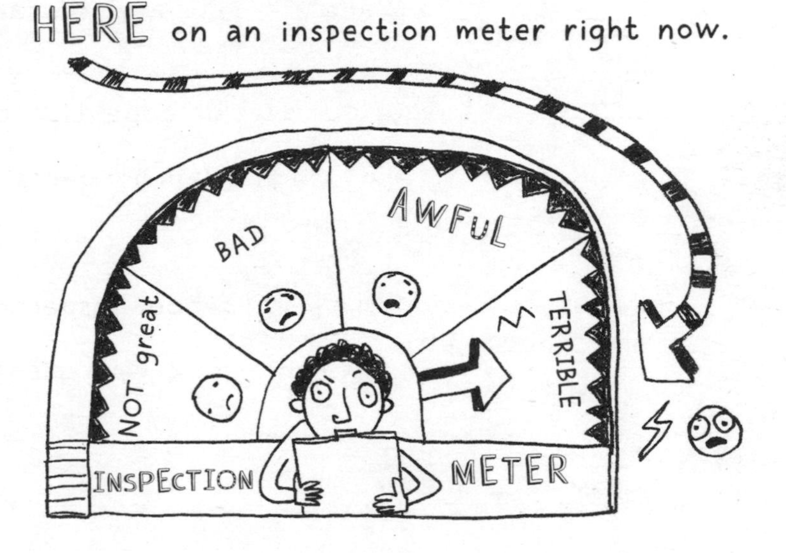

I'm going to have to stay OUT of that inspector's way as much as I can – otherwise his report might end up looking like THIS:

INSPECTION REPORT ON OAKFIELD SCHOOL

This school might have passed its inspection if it weren't for **ONE** boy in particular called TOM GATES who managed to lower the score for EVERYTHING because of his VERY shabby behaviour. WHAT a shame.

Lateness for school	☒	fail
Causing accidents	☒	fail
Pushing into the dinner queue	☒	fail
Drawing funny pictures of inspectors	☒	fail

I concentrate on finishing my delicious pizza while watching Marcus trying to pick off the burnt chocolate raisins from his.

When I leave the dinner hall he's STILL doing it, so I say, EEEEEEWWWWW FLIES! as I walk past because I can tell he's still not sure what they are.

For the rest of lunch break, I hang out with Derek and Solid, and Derek tells us how the filming is going in his class.

"Not bad – we're pretending the TEACHERS get taken over by ALIENS who land on earth disguised as PLANTS."

Which sounds AMAZING.

"Mrs Worthington makes a very good ALIEN, that's for sure."

(I can't wait to see THAT!)

I tell Derek and Solid how I keep seeing that same school inspector all the TIME.

"Which one?" Derek asks.

"The one who was in the dinner hall."

"The lady inspector?" Derek asks.

"No, THIS one." I get out my emergency piece of chalk and do a drawing of him on the ground.

"You know who I mean, the one with the slightly WEIRD hair."

Then I remember my piece of STRING, which is handy.

"You MUST know who it is NOW?" I say. Solid does but Derek still looks a bit confused.

"He's the inspector who looks over his clipboard all the time. The one who got jelly in his lap and has LUMPY hair like that,"

I say, pointing to the string, when a voice behind me says,

"I never thought my hair was LUMPY."

(NOT AGAIN...)

It's the same inspector. "Bad luck, Tom," Derek whispers to me.

(Another thing to add to the school report, then.)

I pick up my string and tell a little kid who's looking at me, "This might look like a piece of string – but it could be a kite." They're not that impressed.

On the way home from school, Derek is LAUGHING a LOT about my chalk drawing.

he says.

Then he suggests, "You should come over to mine. I've got a NEW song for the band."

Which sounds EXCITING.

"And you can see Dad's cat barriers."

(Cat barriers? That sounds interesting too.)

"June's CAT keeps sneaking into the garage and sleeping ZZZZZZZZ on Dad's record collection – it's driving him CRAZY!"

Derek's dad likes to come and listen to us rehearse when we have a band practice. He gives us "tips" on how to perform and play too.

Which Derek **loves** (not).

I rush into my house first just to let Dad know I'm home (and to lOOk for treats. Mmm ... nothing). Then when I get to Derek's house, I see what he means about the

CAT BARRIERS.

THEY'RE EVERYWHERE.

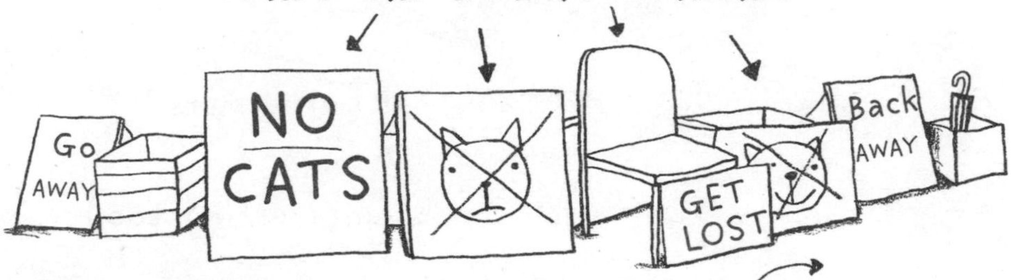

"Are they working?" I ask Derek as I step over them.

"Not really." Then before he plays me my new song I ask him,

"What's it about?"

And he says,

"No, really, what's the song about?"

(Oh, OK. He's not joking. It is a song about a cat.)

Derek's recorded a tune to sing to so I listen.

I'm quiet as a mouse
I make my home in someone else's house
I'm not fussy, any place will do
Go AWAY
If it's warm, I like a place with food
You won't hear me taking a stroll
Straight through the flowers
Jump on a wall
Over the grass I don't care
I'm awake in the dark
And sleep in the day
Where I leave all my FUR
I'll make my home there
Maioww

Mr Fingle suddenly appears and starts clapping his hands and jumping up and down. We both think he just likes Derek's song...

Turns out June's cat has sneaked past the barriers and he's just SHOOOOOOOOINNGGGG him away!

While **M**r Fingle chases the cat over the garden fence. I tell Derek I **love** the song and I'll try and learn it if he sends me a copy. When he comes back **M**r Fingle tells us,

"That cat's got some **NERVE!** You'd think he'd know by now he's **NOT** welcome."

"Cats can't read signs, Dad," Derek says. (It's a good point.)

"Well he won't be back here again," **M**r Fingle tells us confidently.

Not until night-time anyway.

In the morning, thanks to June's cat keeping me awake all night, I'm really tired. And I still have Derek's SONG going ROUND and ROUND in my head.

I'm a cat
I'm a cat

I can't stop singing it either.

"I'm a cat, I'm a cat, don't mess with me!"

"Hey, Tom, you sing like a cat too..."

(Delia's awake then ... groan.)

"Sorry, Tom – I take that back," she adds (suspiciously). "A cat sounds a LOT better than you do."

"Morning, Delia – are you still grounded then?" I remind her (because she's being annoying).

"No, not any more, you'll be pleased to hear." I am – she won't be in the house bugging me, which is good.

I go downstairs and Mum's already gone to work early. I'm hoping she's left me a nice packed lunch. That way I can avoid eating in the dinner hall today until ALL the school inspectors have **gone**.

I spot a note on the fridge that looks promising.

Fingers crossed Mum put a treat inside for me. I take a look and there's ... NOTHING. So I check round the whole kitchen in all the usual places Mum hides the treats, just in case.

Teapot? No. Behind the tins? No. The last place I look is in the real biscuit tin. I've only gone and found a **CARAMEL WAFER**.

This is a good start to my day.

Derek's waiting for me outside already.

"Guess what?" I say.

"What, Tom?"

"I have a CARAMEL WAFER in my lunch box today."

Just saying the words CARAMEL WAFER makes me want to eat it.

As we walk to school I take out the wafer and look at it.

"Let's have it NOW," I say to Derek.

"Isn't it for your lunch?" he asks me.

"Yes – but I can't wait." Then I carefully unwrap the wafer and split it in half.

I give one bit to Derek and the other bit's for me.

Then to make the wafer last a bit longer I split up the layers and eat the chocolate off the outside as well.

"This works with custard creams too," I tell Derek.

He says,

"Do you think we might be a bit LATE?"

It's really quiet everywhere.

"We're not late," I tell Derek confidently.

"We've got

LOADS

of time."

"YOU'RE LATE, TOM!"

Mr Fullerman tells me as I run into class.

Sorry, sir, I say and sit down.

AMY looks at me and pulls a face.

"What have you been eating, Tom? It's all round your mouth."

(Must be the caramel wafer.)

Marcus starts looking at me too. He says.

"EEEEWWWW."

I try and ignore him.

If I were at home I'd pick off the crumbs and eat them.

But with AMY, Marcus and Mr Fullerman looking at me, I wipe them away and just scatter the crumbs around my table a bit.

I find myself moving the crumbs into a pattern ...

... and write my name in them.

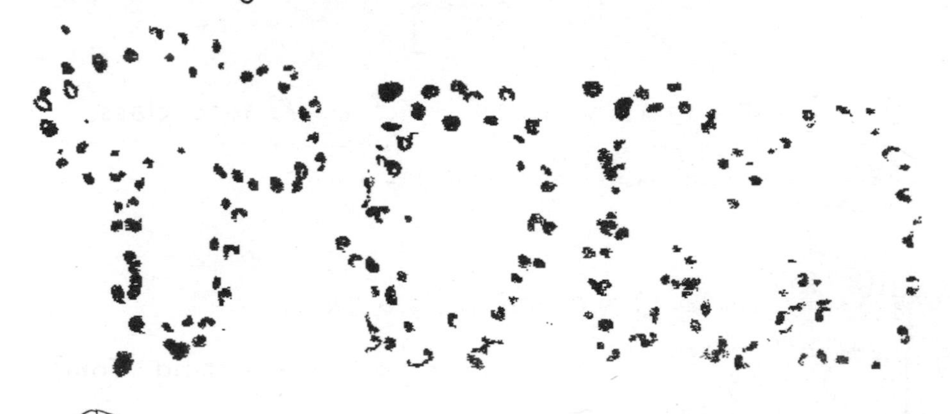

"That's disgusting, Tom," AMY says.

"EEEEWWWW."

(It's not like I'm going to eat them or anything.)

It's not the BEST start to the day,

it does get (a tiny bit) better.

1. I get TWO questions RIGHT in our maths quiz – which is good for me. (Marcus gets ONE right ... and one wrong.)

2. I manage to avoid all contact with any of the school inspectors for the WHOLE day.

(It was a mission.)

3. At lunchtime I discover a CEREAL BAR that Mum gave me in my lunch box. It's not *THAT* much of a treat but it's better than nothing.

Cereal Bar

Derek's class have finished making their ALIEN film about the teachers. Which got me thinking (and doodling) right at the end of my English lesson with Mr Fullerman. What if ...

It's a funny end to my day.

If I had my own lucky meter it would be here right now, because I've had quite a few lucky escapes. (Which doesn't happen all the time – THAT'S for sure.)

The first lucky escape happened when I woke up at seven o'clock this morning (for a change). I went downstairs for breakfast, then spotted Mum's "TO DO" LIST  stuck on the fridge.

THIS was written at the top.

URGENT

MUST TAKE TOM TO BUY SENSIBLE SCHOOL SHOES.

Really? If I had my OWN "TO DO" LIST, sensible-shoe shopping with Mum would definitely NOT be on it. ☹

But finding the list early meant I could make a few changes. Like rubbing out sensible-shoe shopping for a start.

URGENT
MUST TAKE TOM TO BUY SENSIBLE SCHOOL SHOES.
ALSO BUY:
Toothpaste
Foil
Shampoo
A4 paper
Envelopes
FAKE TAN – FOR EXTRA GLOW
Washing powder
Healthy snacks for Tom's lunch box
Cereal bars
Apples

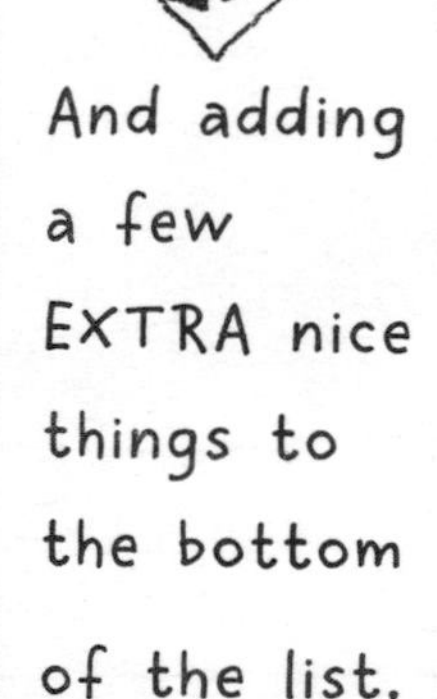

And adding a few EXTRA nice things to the bottom of the list. ☺

Though I had a feeling Mum might notice some of the changes I'd made. It looked a bit messy.

URGENT
MUST TAKE TOM TO BUY SWEETS

ALSO BUY:
Toothpaste
Foil
Shampoo
A4 paper
Envelopes
FAKE TAN – FOR EXTRA GLOW
Washing powder
Healthy snacks for Tom's lunch box
Cereal bars
Apples
Caramel wafers
TREATS (any kind)

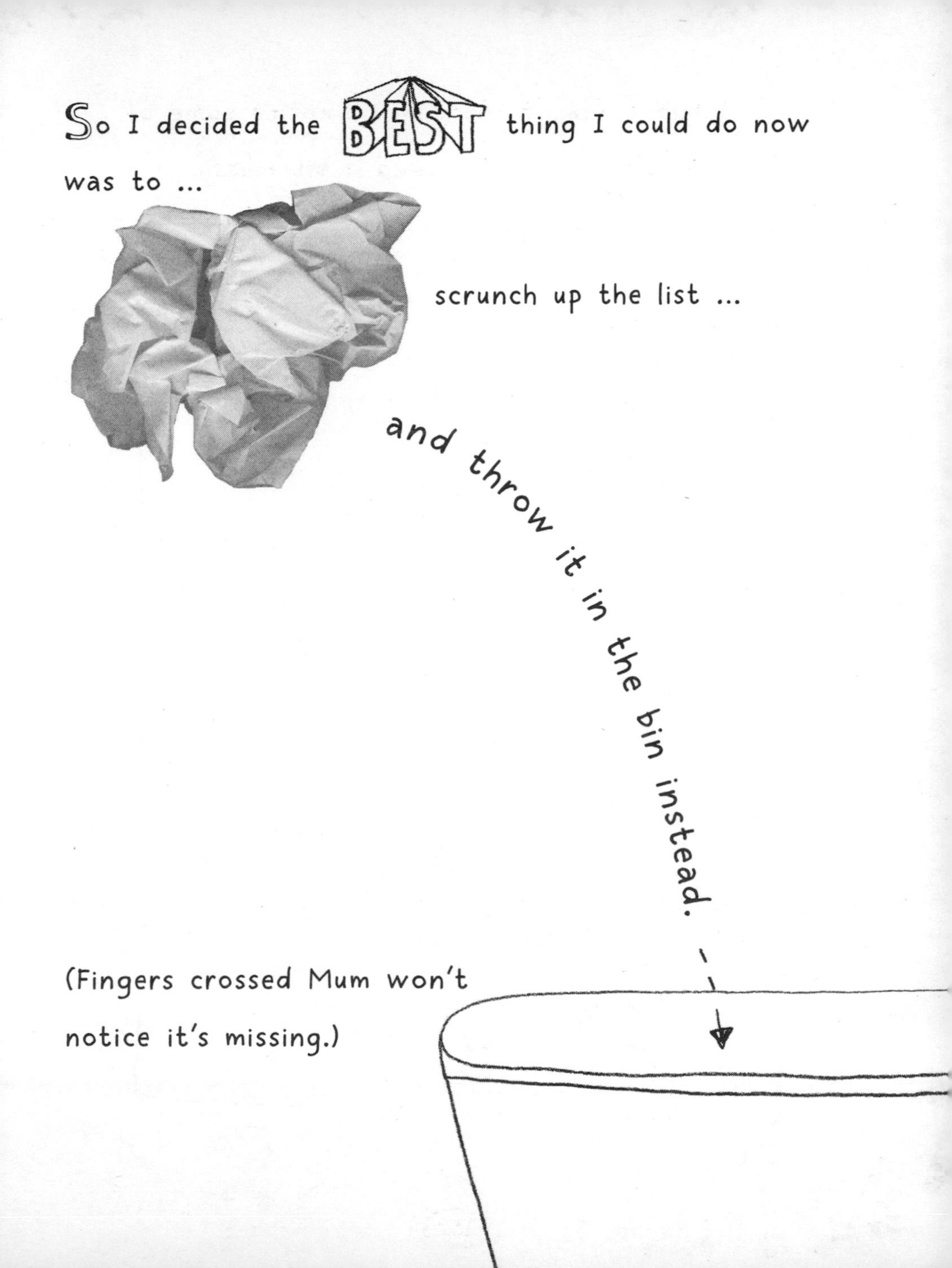

So I decided the BEST thing I could do now was to ...

scrunch up the list ...

and throw it in the bin instead.

(Fingers crossed Mum won't notice it's missing.)

But the **first** thing Mum says when she comes downstairs is,

"Where's my list gone?"

Huh? What list? I say.

Which is a combination of pretending **not** to know about Mum's list and having a MOUTH full of cereal.

"I'm sure I left it on the fridge?" she adds, looking around.

THEN Mum only goes and says, "Never mind, I think I can remember what was on it."

(Oh NO, I wasn't expecting that.)

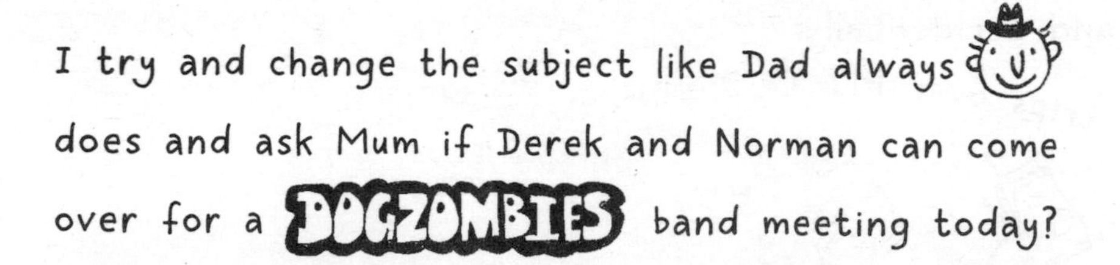

I try and change the subject like Dad always does and ask Mum if Derek and Norman can come over for a **DOGZOMBIES** band meeting today?

Mum doesn't say no, which is a good sign.

So I QUICKLY go and call them to see if they're free.

When Derek answers, he says he wants to come round NOW because his mum wants him to tidy his room.

Tidy your room

"She might forget about it if I come over to yours," he says. (I'm not so sure.)

Norman's still asleep, so I'll call him back later.

I go back to the kitchen and Mum's already writing out A NEW LIST. I can't see anything like shoe shopping on it, which is a relief.

Everything's going fine – until Derek arrives and accidentally trips over MY OLD SCHOOL shoes

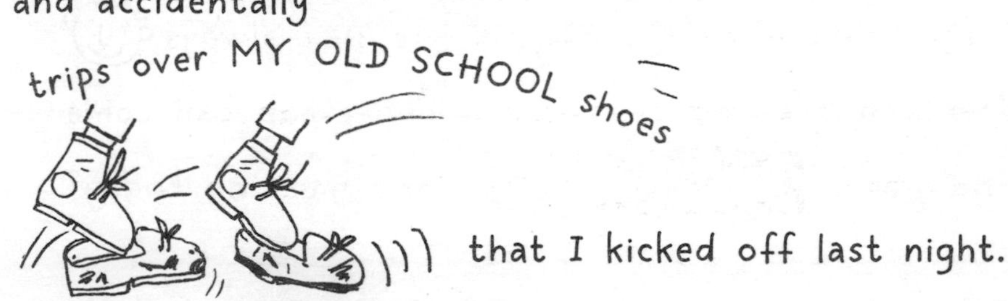

that I kicked off last night.

The shoes JOG Mum's memory.

"NOW I REMEMBER! Look at your SHOES! We MUST get you a new pair today, Tom," she says. groan

"And what's all this white stuff inside? It looks like flour. Did YOU spill that flour, Tom?"

(I keep quiet and shrug my sholders.) Derek mouths sorry to me, but it's not his fault.

I remind Mum that I can't go shoe shopping, as I've got friends with me.

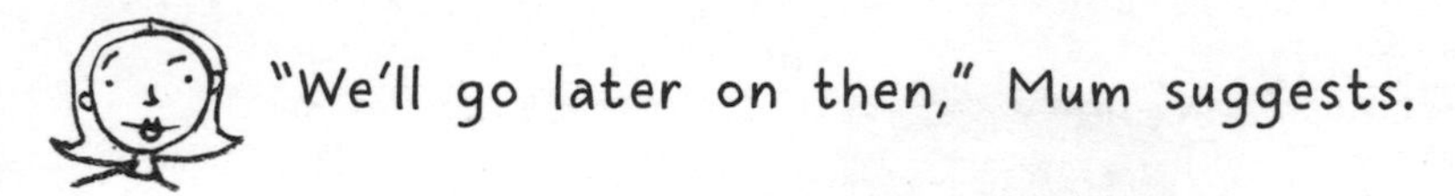

"We'll go later on then," Mum suggests.

"Norman's coming over too. I really can't go," I say again in case she didn't hear me.

(Mum's idea of sensible shoes is bound to be different to mine.)

THOSE ARE NICE

NERD

I tell Mum that... "We have a VERY important BAND PRACTICE and it's going to last for AGES! Won't it, Derek? "

It will, Mrs Gates, Derek agrees.

"We need LOTS of practice - don't we, Derek?"

Derek nods.

Then Dad comes into the kitchen to make some tea, followed by Delia (who ignores me, and everyone else).

Mum's still wafting my shoes around, saying,

"You CAN'T go to school in these, Tom. They're falling to PIECES!"

"Aren't we all!" Dad laughs.

"Speak for yourself!" Mum gives Dad a stare and raises her eyebrow.

Then she looks at me and says,

"I'll just have to get you a nice STRONG, sensible pair of shoes myself." Luckily Mum then gets distracted by Delia leaving her dirty plate and mug in the sink.

"Let's go and call Norman," I whisper to Derek. So we sneak out of the kitchen and this time he's awake. He says he's on his way over.

Yeah

Derek seems pleased. But that's mostly because of the MONEY he's just found in his POCKET!

"Let's go to the shop and get something NICE," he suggests, which is a great idea.

I tell Mum and Dad we're going to the shop so FAST that they don't have a chance to ask for (Milk?) or anything else.

(like they normally do).

As we're heading towards the shop, we BUMP right into NORMAN. When I say we "BUMP", what I really mean is he LEAPS OUT at us from behind a bus shelter and says,

It takes us a while to calm down. Norman's holding a copy of a DOCTOR PLANET book, so I ask him, "Is that book SCARY?"

"Not really – but I did get these FREE with it." He turns his back on us, then spins round wearing these ...

(I'm not sure Norman looks that different? But I don't say that.)

Derek thinks he's got enough money to buy fruit chews for all of us.

Which is nice of him. ☺

But in the shop, people keep staring at us, which is ODD – until I see what Norman's doing NOW.

"It's a good look for you, Norman." I tell him.

THANKS!

The fruit chews have put us all in a very good mood for band practice.

We walk past the bus shelter (again) and THIS TIME we notice a BIG poster for the BAND BATTLE competition.

(Norman LEAPT out at us before.)

"LOOK." Derek points.

"It's a sign – we could WIN it!" Norman says (through his T-shirt).

"Do you think everyone else who sees the poster will think that too?" I wonder.

We take turns in standing in front of the poster and pretending the crowd are cheering for US. Then Derek looks closely at the small writing on the poster and says:

"PLEASE FILL IN THE APPLICATION AND SEND IT, ALONG WITH ONE TRACK FROM YOUR BAND, BY THE END OF THIS MONTH AT THE LATEST. NO ENTRIES WILL BE ACCEPTED AFTER THIS DATE."

"Isn't it the end of the month in ... TWO DAYS' TIME?" Derek asks. (He's right.)

"Not long then?" I say.

Norman's not really taking much notice. He's looking at the ground.

SOMEONE is wearing the POINTIEST shoes I've ever seen. They're SO pointy they're sticking out from under the bus shelter.

"LOOK!"

Norman whispers a bit loudly.

"Watch this!"

Then before we can stop him, the pointy shoes suddenly have ...

... a pair of

STICK-ON EYES.

We're trying not to LAUGH when the pointy shoes start MOVING! We turn around and run really fast in the other direction. We don't stop until we get to my house.

"I'd love to know who wears pointy shoes like that?" I say, slightly out of breath.

"They'll be wondering where the eyes came from!" Derek says to Norman, who's busy looking for other places to stick his eyes.

I need to find my guitar for band practice, so we pop into my house FIRST.

"Turn on the TV if you want. I won't be too long," I tell Derek and Norman. But when I come back they're just sitting there looking at THIS NOTE.

"Sorry - that's my mum. She's the TV police," I tell them.

(Groan.)

All that running away from pointy shoes has made us thirsty. "Let's NIP to the kitchen and get some water," I suggest, then add, "I'd offer you a SNACK if I could find them."

"I can see some!" Norman says.

"Me too!" Derek shouts.

Sure enough, there's a whole packet of wafers on top of the kitchen cupboard.

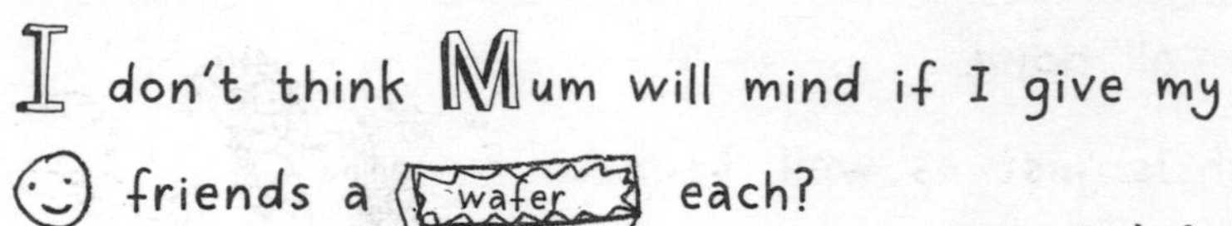

(She's always telling me TREATS are for guests.)

Well that's what I'm going to say if she finds out. I take the wafers down and I'm about to hand them out when I have an IDEA.

"If we do the wafer biscuit trick*, Mum won't spot that they've gone (for a while)."

So that's what we do.

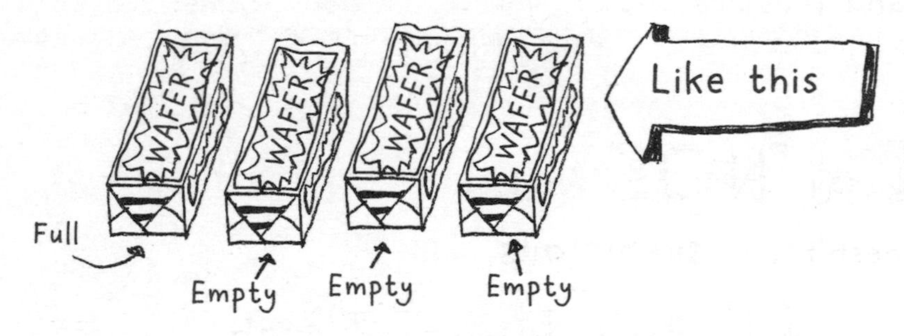

I take three wafers out and leave the empty wrappers. I carefully put them back where they came from.

*See p. 43, *The Brilliant World of Tom Gates*, for how to do the wafer biscuit trick.

There – all done.

Which is just as well, because as we're finishing the last bits of wafer, Mum comes in and starts chatting.

"Hello, boys. Now, Tom, are you SURE you don't want to come with me to buy your lovely new school shoes?"

"No, Mum – I'm sure." (She's being embarrassing.)

"OK – it's a bit early, but as you've got a band practice, would you all like a caramel wafer?"

(WHAT?)

I say "NO!" first, then "YES!" so Mum doesn't get suspicious.

"I'll get them!" I shout.

Mum laughs. "Trust YOU to know where they are, Tom!" (Whoops ... oh well.)

Derek and Norman watch me bring the wafers down. I take them off the shelf REALLY carefully so I don't **SQUASH** the EMPTY ones (all three of them).

I hand out a wafer each, and keep one for myself. We all hold them really gently (which is not easy to do, especially for Norman).

Mum says, "I'll have one too if there's a spare." Luckily there's one real wafer left.

Mum starts eating hers and wonders why we're not eating ours.

"That's not like you, Tom – aren't they your favourite?"

"We're saving them," I explain.

"For band practice at Derek's. We're leaving now," I add so we can go.

I grab my guitar and keep holding on to my wafer right up until we get to Derek's garage.

"That was LUCKY," Derek says. Norman's wrapper got SQUASHED while he was SQUEEZING past a cat barrier.

We haven't even started listening to Derek's song or practising when Mr Fingle appears and says,

"If you see that cat, will you SHHHOOOOO it away?"

"Yes, Dad," Derek says.

"Is this a DOGZOMBIES band practice?"

"Sort of," I tell him. "We're entering the BAND BATTLE competition."

("Here we go," Derek whispers.)

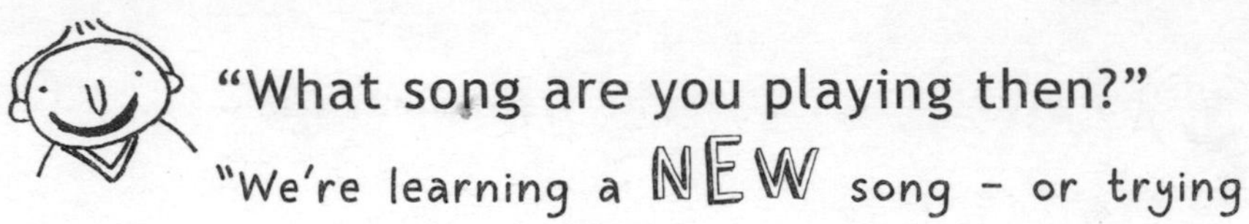

"What song are you playing then?"

"We're learning a NEW song – or trying to," Derek tells him.

"Derek's written a song about a CAT – it's really good!" I say.

"It's NOT finished yet," Derek adds.

"And the audition's in TWO DAYS so we need to send off a recording of it."

Huh?

Norman seems surprised. "TWO DAYS?"

Mr Fingle is shaking his head.

"Playing a NEW song could be risky. I'd stick to one you all know. I can help you record it if you want?"

(It kind of makes sense?)

"We'll do my cat song another time," Derek says.

"WILD THING!"

Norman shouts – which is a good idea.

 "Always a CLASSIC!" Mr Fingle tells us.

(True.)

So – "WILD THING" it is.

We're about to have a practice when Mr Fingle starts "SSSShhhhhing" again.

He creeps over to the door.

"LOOK! It's that cat again..."

I can't see anything yet – but the door starts to open very slowly and Mr Fingle gets ready to

Shhhoooooo it away.

"We're trying to have a BAND PRACTICE here, Dad!" Derek says.

His dad whispers. "I think it's..."

What's HE doing here?

Mr Fingle stops shushing cats in time to say,

"They were just about to play 'WILD THING'."

My dad says he's come round to "help us" (well, that's what he says). But every time we try to practice, Mr Fingle and Dad start chatting about what song they'd play if it was them auditioning for BAND BATTLE.

"Err, hello? Our band practice?" Derek tells them.

"We need to record this song and send it off," he adds.

Then Dad reminds us that we have a recording already. "Remember?" (I don't.)

"I can send that off for you I'd you'd like," he tells us. OK, Dad.

Which seems like a good idea, especially as Mr Fingle has **moved** on to talking about June's cat.

"He almost ruined a

WHOLE box of records!

"That cat's been in our garden too," Dad starts telling him.

Norman is doing RANDOM **drumming** now, which means no one hears the door start to open again.

And this time it really is...

JUNE'S DAD

What's he doing here?

"Sorry to bother you, but June says our CAT might have sneaked into your house. He's been wandering around a lot, I'm afraid."

Straight away Mr Fingle rushes off to check his records. (There's no sign of a cat, which is a relief.)

Phew

"Thanks for checking," June's dad says. Then he looks around and asks, "Are you boys in a band, then?"

"Yes - we're called DOGZOMBIES," I tell him.

"I used to be in a band too," June's dad says.

My dad and Mr Fingle both say, "What band were you in, then?"

(We're listening too.)

"I doubt you'd have heard of us. We were around in the 90s playing rock."

"I'm a HUGE 90s rock fan," Mr Fingle says.

"What was the band called?"  Dad asks.

PLASTIC CUP.

Which makes both our dads go REALLY!

"I've got all your albums!"

(I've NEVER heard of **PLASTIC CUP**.)

"Dad's going to start playing them. We'll have to listen to a WHOLE album if we stay here," Derek warns us.

My dad and Mr Fingle are a bit OVEREXCITED to be meeting a member of PLASTIC CUP. Even if it IS just June's dad (which is weird).

"We might as well go to your place now, Tom?" Derek says. Which is a good idea because we can watch THE CRAZY FRUIT BUNCH. Mum won't tell me to turn the TV off if I have friends with me.

We leave the dads all talking about the ALBUM COVER. Which as far as I can see is just a plastic cup?

Dad promises to send off our track for the BAND BATTLE audition when he gets home.

"I can't believe he was in Plastic Cup!" he whispers to me.

"OK, Dad ... calm down," I tell him.

Me, Norman and Derek leave them all to it. And we accidentally leave the garage door open as well...

The first thing I have to do is take down Mum's note that's stuck to the TV.

Then I turn on THE CRAZY FRUIT BUNCH.

Normans jumps up to help himself to the fruit bowl on the table. "We're a bit like The Crazy Fruit Bunch, aren't we?" he says, putting the fruit on his head.

Derek joins in, and I do as well, when the doorbell rings. I go to answer it (still balancing the fruit).

It's JUNE?

(I would have taken the fruit off my head if I'd known it was her.)

"Is my dad here?" she asks me.

"Err, no, he's next door at Derek's. We're watching

" I tell her, trying to explain the fruit. "Have you seen it?"

"No, Tom. Thanks, I'll go next door then."

She peers into the house and catches sight of Derek and Norman.

"It's a 

funny cartoon," I tell her.

"I'll take your word for it."

(I forgot she doesn't have a TV.)

June's about to leave when Mum comes down to see who it is.

"Hello, June - have you come round to play?"

(Mum just said "PLAY" ... groan.)

"I'm just looking for my dad, thanks," June tells her.

"Well, you're **VERY** welcome to come round anytime. Isn't she, Tom?"

I nod - and a banana falls off my head.

I manage to close the door and wave goodbye to June just in time, before Mum *Whips* out a bag and says ...

"I was SO LUCKY to get these for you" and shows me

A **MASSIVE chunky** PAIR OF SHOES.

"I hope they fit," Mum says. (I hope they don't.)

"You can watch more cartoons if you try them on, Tom."

(Mmmm ... OK then.) Here goes.

Sadly - they fit.

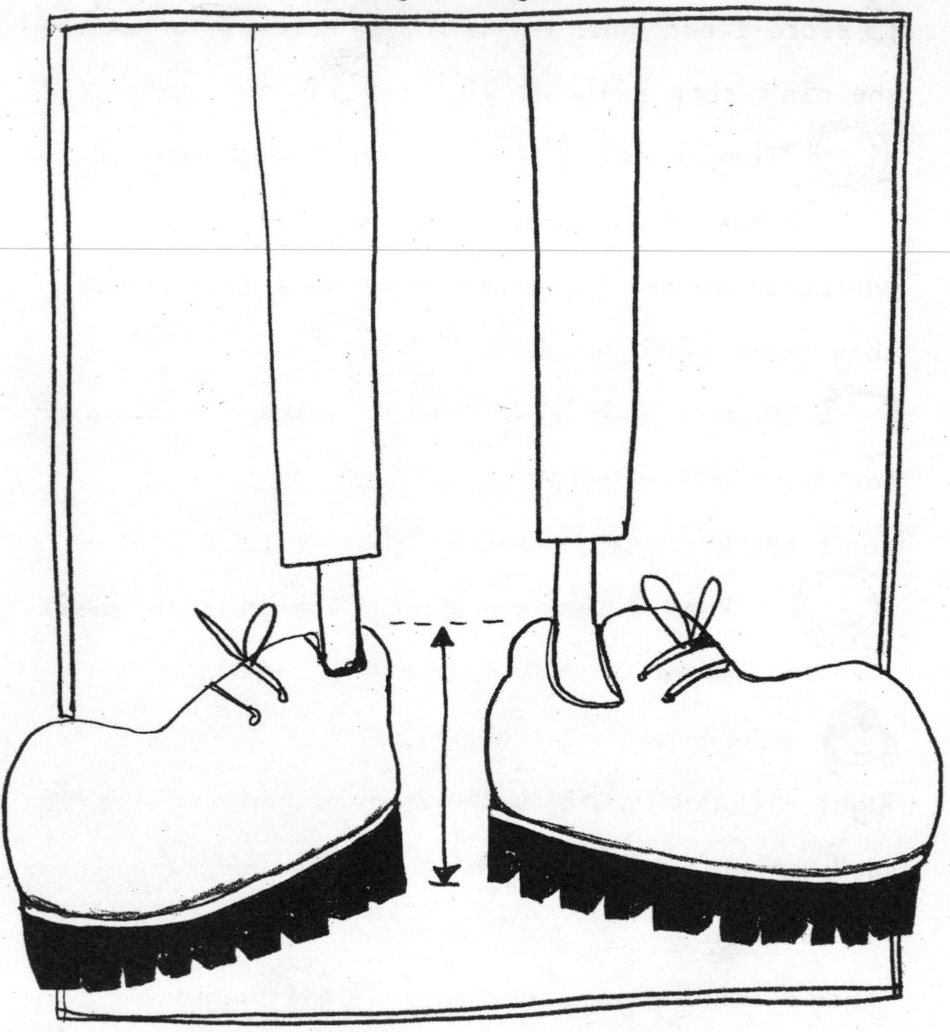

But I look like a CLOWN!

Mum says they'll last for ages. (I'm not wearing them to school. NO WAY.)

Before I can take them off, Delia sees me and she can't stop LAUGHING. Ha! Ha! Ha! Ha!

"They're not THAT funny, Delia," Mum says.

Derek and Norman have come out to see what's going on. I can tell from their faces what they think of my shoes. Ha! He! He!

"I can't wear them, Mum - besides, they're too tight." (They're actually quite comfy but I don't tell her that.)

"Really? That's a shame. They're such good sturdy school shoes, Tom."

Delia laughs even more. "STURDY and MASSIVE." Right - that's it, I'm taking them off. Mum says she'll try and take the shoes back to the shop if she can. "Or you'll have to wear them."

"They'd make a good doorstop," Delia laughs.

My shoe humiliation is almost worth it, as we get to watch a lot more of THE CRAZY FRUIT BUNCH.

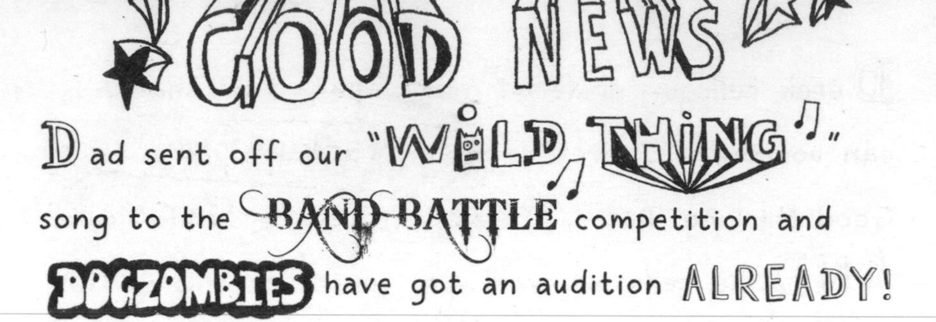

Dad sent off our "WILD THING" song to the BAND BATTLE competition and DOGZOMBIES have got an audition ALREADY!

"It's tomorrow after school, Tom," Dad tells me at breakfast.

"That was QUICK!" I say.

"They know a good band when they hear it," he says, smiling at me.

There's not much time to get nervous (even though I will). That's what I tell Derek on our way to school.

He says, "Great – not wearing your NEW shoes then?"

"NEVER!" I say, shaking my head.

"They did make me LAUGH, though!"

"Exactly – that's why I'm never wearing them!"

Derek tells me that he has a spare pair that I can borrow if I ever need a backup plan.

Good thinking, Derek. (That's why he's my BEST MATE!)

AND he tells me we'll get to watch the ALIEN film his class made this week too.

It's quite funny. But the REALLY

GOOD NEWS IS ...
THE INSPECTORS HAVE GONE

AT LAST! HOORAY!

It's easy to tell they've left because Mr Fullerman isn't wearing his bow tie any more and the teachers are more relaxed. sigh

Mr Fullerman wants to know if everyone has their SIGNED reading diaries today.

Marcus says "YES" really loudly and AMY has hers too. I have mine, but I might need to add another "signature" to it?

(I'll do it at breaktime when no one's looking.)

After ENRICHMENT WEEK, going back to doing maths means I have to CONCENTRATE.

Groan.

Which is tricky when I keep thinking about THE AUDITION tomorrow (and a few other things too).

I still have my string, so I fiddle with that while answering the questions on my maths worksheet.

(I wish I had one box of chocolates right now. Mmmmm.)

MATHS WORKSHEET

Q1 John has bought **25** boxes of chocolates and there are **36** chocolates in each box. How many chocolates did John buy?

A LOT!

mmmm chocolates →

$25 \times 36 =$?

900? (I think)

It's a struggle, but I manage to get the worksheet done. And add a sneaky signature to my reading diary too. Not bad for a morning's work. ☺

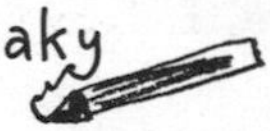

I'm thinking about doing another string doodle ...

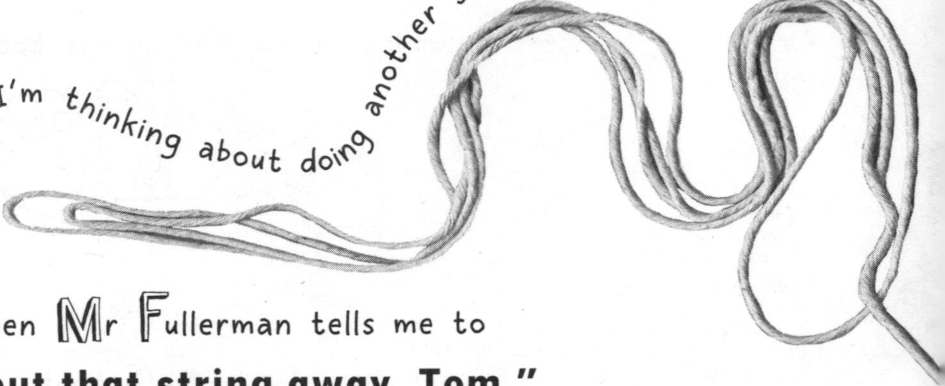

when Mr Fullerman tells me to

"put that string away, Tom."

Yes, sir. (That was close...)

"Now, everyone, pay attention,"

Mr Fullerman says to the class.

(I'm hoping it's not another maths worksheet.) ☹

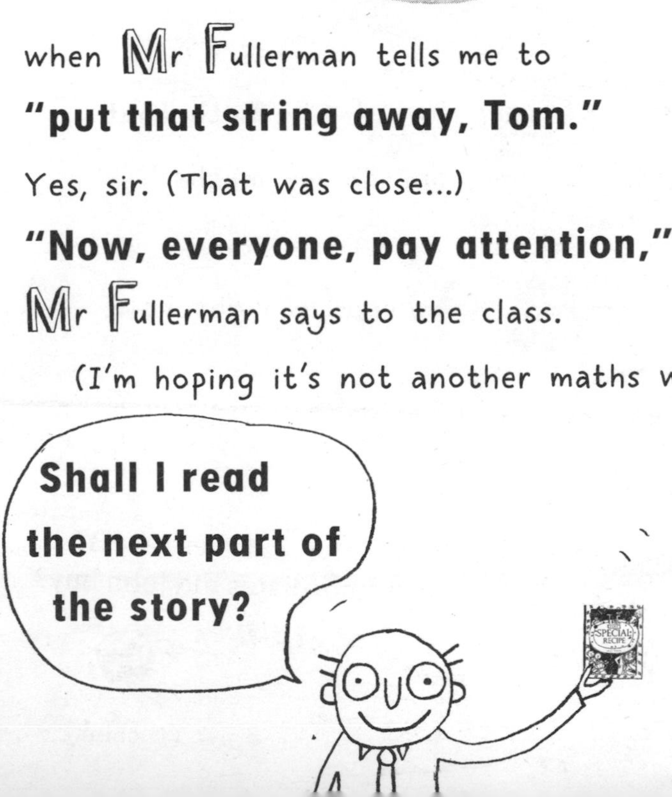
Shall I read the next part of the story?
SPECIAL RECIPE

YES!

I do an air punch too.

Air punch

CHAPTER 2

Mayor Cuthbert Bottle checked himself in the mirror. **"Well look at ME,"** he said, smoothing down an eyebrow with his manicured finger. **"Don't I look absolutely . . . GORGEOUS."** The mayor patted his strange puffy hair, which moved ever so slightly to the right and then to the left.

He stared at the two food inspectors, who were standing behind him in their white coats. **"Don't you both agree?"** he asked them.

Walter and Roger gulped. Was this a trick question? The WRONG answer would put the mayor in a bad mood all day and they didn't want THAT to happen.

Walter took a deep breath. **"Yes, Mayor, you look very handsome indeed,"** he said.

"I agree," Roger added. **"What a great suit you have on, and your HAIR, oh your HAIR"** — Roger paused as he searched for the RIGHT words to use — **"well, it has never looked so unbelievably . . .**

... FLUFFY!" he said excitedly.

The mayor seemed pleased with both their answers (which was a relief). **"Tell me, are there any PRESS photographers lurking outside in the bushes waiting to take a SNEAKY picture of me?"** he wondered.

"Absolutely NOT, Mayor Bottle. We made sure no one from the press would be snooping around until EVERYTHING had gone EXACTLY to plan."

"And has EVERYTHING gone to plan?" the mayor asked while trying to look them BOTH in the eye (which wasn't easy to do, since he was a very short man).

"Yes, Mayor, it's ALL gone EXACTLY to plan." BOTH the food inspectors crossed their fingers behind their backs and smiled nervously.

"Well, may I suggest then..." the mayor said calmly, **"THAT YOU GET THOSE PHOTOGRAPHERS BACK HERE RIGHT NOW!"** he SHOUTED (not so calmly).

I love a
PLAN

"I want to see PICTURES of ME looking fantastic!

I want HEADLINES in ALL the papers that say:

BUG-INFESTED TEA SHOP CLOSED DOWN AT LAST!
REPLACED BY LUXURY SKYSCRAPER BOTTLE TOWERS!"

The mayor was yelling and waving his arms around SO DRAMATICALLY that the small squirrel asleep on top of his head almost woke up. (Nobody EVER mentioned the mayor's VERY odd hairstyle – not to his face, anyway. For some reason the mayor thought his hair looked more "natural" with the odd combover – but as YOU can see, it really didn't.)

"Yes, Mayor!" Walter and Roger said while moving swiftly into action. **"We'll do that right away."**

"Let me know when the photographers arrive so I can pretend to be SURPRISED," the mayor said while checking himself in the mirror again.

You might have gathered already (unless you haven't BEEN PAYING ATTENTION!) that Mayor Cuthbert Bottle wasn't a very nice person. The mayor came from a REALLY long line of ROTTEN RELATIVES, so it was hardly surprising that he turned out to be so mean.

His own parents were not exactly a loveable couple. Mr and Mrs Bottle made no secret of the fact that from the moment their baby son was born, they had both felt deeply and UTTERLY ...

disappointed.

"He's not much of a looker, is he?" Mrs Bottle said while staring at her son.

"He takes after you then,"

Mr Bottle laughed back.

"What shall we call him, apart from facially challenged?" Mrs Bottle wondered.

"With THAT face, we'd better call him something ridiculous so he learns to stick up for himself FAST," Mr Bottle said.

So they gave their son the silliest name they could think of: Cuthbert Banjo Baby Bottle. And it didn't take long for Cuthbert Bottle to learn the rotten ways of his parents. He went from being a slightly pleasant baby to a hideous teenager, who grew up to be a vain and vile man.

(You get the picture.)

And as Cuthbert got older, he became quite successful in business by lying, bribing and cheating his way right to the TOP of the ladder.

Cuthbert loved the thrill of POWER. And after a few dodgy deals with a little bit of VOTE fixing (OK, a LOT of vote fixing), Cuthbert eventually managed to become the MAYOR of the whole city.

But having a fancy title and wearing a fabulous CHAIN of office wasn't enough for Cuthbert. He was very greedy and wanted MORE (much more). It was after reading a FLASHY magazine about RICH and powerful people that he announced,

"I want a HUGE SKYSCRAPING TOWER full of LUXURY SHOPS and APARTMENTS with MY VERY OWN NAME EMBLAZONED ON EVERY FLOOR."

(The BOTTLE – not the Cuthbert name – in case you were wondering.)

Mayor Bottle dreamt of living right at the top of this tower, where he could look down on everyone else in the city. (Remember, he was a very short man, so looking down on people other than children wasn't something he did very often.)

"I want to BUILD BOTTLE TOWERS RIGHT HERE," the mayor said, thinking everything was going to be all easy peasy. Then he gave the order to buy EVERY building that was in his way.

But not everyone wanted to sell. So he pretended the buildings were FALLING DOWN, which almost worked. There was only ONE building that didn't want to move or sell. And that was THE TEA SHOP.

Mr and Mrs Crumble didn't believe their shop was falling down. Besides, it was their home and where would they go?

Mayor Bottle was FURIOUS with the Crumbles. He wanted them OUT. So he hatched a plan and rubbed his hands together at the thought of what was about to happen. If his plan worked, this would be the last day THE TEA SHOP would EVER be open.

"I'm fed up of that sickly-sweet family and their hideous children Apple and Plum. They're going to be TOAST today!" he laughed to himself. (In other words, Mayor Bottle had found a way of KICKING them out of THE TEA SHOP for good.)

Ha Ha!

The mayor double-checked with the food inspectors again. **"Do you have the CONDEMNED NOTICE and compulsory purchase order?"**

"Yes, Mayor Bottle – we do." Roger waved some bits of official-looking paper around.

"I want to SEE THOSE Crumbles ... CRUMBLE!"

The mayor laughed at his own joke and the inspectors laughed with him to keep him happy.

"Then what are we waiting for? I'm ready for my close-up." Mayor Bottle took one more look in the mirror, then stepped outside.

(He was good at pretending to be surprised by photographers.)

CHAPTER 3

In THE TEA SHOP, Mr and Mrs Crumble and their children Apple and Plum were arranging the very last plate of cakes on a beautiful stand. SOMEHOW they had managed the impossible task of cleaning up THE TEA SHOP and making a whole new batch of cakes and biscuits before the mayor and his inspectors were due to arrive.

EVERYONE was EXHAUSTED, but the whole place looked sparkling and almost like nothing had ever happened. There hadn't been enough time to make every kind of bread and cake again. But there were plenty of chocolate brownies. Mr Crumble looked around. **"Are we ready?"** he asked.

"As ready as we'll ever be," Mrs Crumble said nervously.

"STOP!" shouted Apple.

She ran across the tearoom and without hesitating, she **STAMPED** her foot down on the ground.

There was a CRUNCHING sound, and then Apple moved her shoe.

"Got it!" she said, looking at the squashed bug.

"Get a napkin QUICKLY and wipe it up. Be careful not to leave anything on the floor – no legs, arms or bits of body. OK?" Mrs Crumble told her.

Apple cleaned up the bug and just in time, because outside they could hear the vans and cars that belonged to Mayor Cuthbert Bottle, and his team of food inspectors, arriving.

"If this doesn't work, we could lose the shop," Mr Crumble said.

"It will work," Mrs Crumble assured him as she turned the CLOSED sign on THE TEA SHOP door to say OPEN and they all waited for the mayor to come inside.

Mr Fullerman SLAMS the book shut.

"SIR! What happens in the rest of the story?" Brad Galloway asks.

"This book's in the library if you want to read the ending. OR I can read the rest to you another time?"

We all say ... "YEAAHHH!"

"He's in a good mood," I say to AMY.

"All the teachers are, now the inspectors have gone." (True.)

We all go out to break and I look round to see if I can spot Norman so I can remind him about tomorrow's audition. (Even though I called him, he might have forgotten.)

Derek comes with me.

"I think I can see him over there," he says.

It *looks* like Norman. He's busy swinging around on the climbing frame with both arms. Right up until he sees us and waves ...

and lets go.

(Which is a mistake.)

Norman's on the ground ... but says he's FINE.

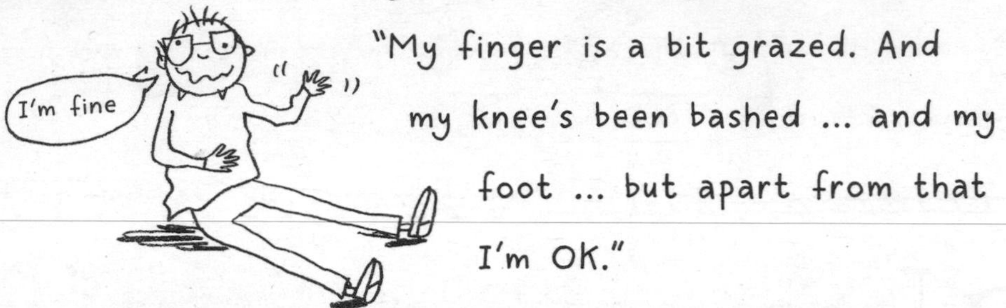

"My finger is a bit grazed. And my knee's been bashed ... and my foot ... but apart from that I'm OK."

"We've got our BAND BATTLE audition tomorrow – are you all right?" Derek asks him.

"Of course! Don't panic, we'll be GREAT!" Then Norman gets up and swings around a bit more.

I remind him (AGAIN) just in case.

"We'll meet up and go to my house after school tomorrow – OK, Norman?"

He says, What for? (like he's forgotten)

then Only joking!

(Very funny, Norman.)

I'm having a nice dream about a GIANT CARAMEL WAFER when it starts to feel like someone is SHAKING me.

When I OPEN my eyes,

I see Delia.

"What have you done to MY CLOTHES? They're all covered in FUR and it's making my eyes

WATER!"

Huh?

Delia does look like she's been rolled in FUR (that's suspiciously the same colour as June's cat).

"Did you let that cat into my room?"

"No!" I tell her (but I'm not totally sure?). She **STOMPS** out, so I get up and get dressed quickly in case she decides to ***STOMP*** back in again.

Then I *nip* downstairs, only to find ANOTHER TRICKY situation.

There's a note on the NEW school shoes Mum bought for me. She really wants me to wear them.

Dad's already up and he says, "They're not THAT bad, Tom. Better than your old shoes?"

Tom - Please wear them to school. I can't take them back! Mum

(I don't think so.)

"Besides, you don't have another decent pair, do you?"

That's where he's WRONG.

"I have a pair of backup shoes at Derek's," I tell Dad.

"Oh, OK," he says.

"I'll wear them today. They're proper school shoes."

"Well, as long as they fit you and Derek doesn't mind."

"We're the same size," I tell Dad confidently.

But it turns out Derek's backup shoes are a tiny bit ... **snug.** I just say, "Thanks, Derek" and keep that to myself. (They do look better than my old pair.) At least I've remembered to bring my swimming kit for PE today.

And some shampoo.

Normally I wouldn't bother with washing my hair, but as we've got the audition after school, I thought I'd try to scrub up. (And Amy told me I still had white powdery stuff on my head the other day – which I'm guessing was flour – bit embarrassing.)

As I'm walking to school, I discover that Derek's backup shoes are a bit more than **SNUG!** They're rubbing the back of my heels so I walk slowly (which helps).

"All set for the audition tonight?" Derek asks.

"I'm looking forward to it," I tell him.

(I sort of am. It'll be fine - I hope.)

In class, Mr Fullerman does a *SUPER fast* registration and gets us on to the coach to go swimming in no time at all.

"Get changed as quickly as you can, please," he tells everyone.

Why are school swimming lessons are always such a *RUSH?* Though taking off my backup shoes is a **massive** relief.

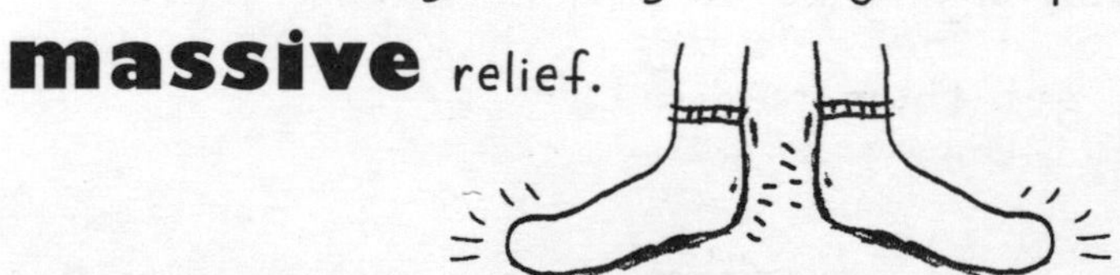

I have my swimming TRUNKS

(which is good)

but I've forgotten my swimming goggles

(which is bad).

I ask, "Has anyone got a spare pair of goggles?"

Marcus is wearing his goggles and he says, "I do, but I'm not allowed to lend them to anyone."

"Thanks for telling me, Marcus."

LUCKILY Solid has a spare pair.  They're a bit BIG and need adjusting, which is tricky. I squeeze them on and it feels like my eyes are popping out of my head now.

Moving them around helps a little, but during the lesson, they keep filling with water  and steaming up.  I spend most of the lesson trying to sort them out! I just get them comfortable ...

... when the lesson's over. I give Solid back his goggles, and he tells me I've been wearing them upside down!

"You've got goggle marks round your eyes now," he adds.

Oh!

"They'll go!" I say confidently. (Well, I hope so.) In the shower I squeeze a big blob of shampoo into my hand.

BLOB

"I think that's suncream, Tom," Solid tells me.

"What?" Great – I must have picked up the wrong

bottle, so I can't wash my own hair now. I wipe the rest of the cream on to my towel.

Then I get dressed and try getting rid of my goggle marks by rubbing my face with my towel.

"You look like a panda, Tom," Marcus tells me on the coach back to school.

(The goggle marks are still there, then.)

"Actually, you look like a red panda. Your face is all red too."

"They're goggle marks and they'll fade," I explain (rubbing them with a towel didn't work then).

"Haven't you got a BAND BATTLE audition later?" he reminds me SMUGLY.

"Yes, DOGZOMBIES got through."

"You might still look like a panda, if those marks don't go."

"They're just goggle marks. They'll go." I'm going to ignore him now.

When we get back to school, other kids start staring at me too.

Even Mr Fullerman asks if I'm feeling OK. "They're just swimming-goggle marks, sir," I tell him as I sit down. Then AMY says I look a bit

BLOTCHY.

"BLOTCHY?"

"Yes – your face looks a funny colour and your hands do too."

I have a closer look and they are a slightly orangey-brown colour. That's odd.

"I'll go and wash it off – it's nothing," I say. Only it doesn't wash off and by the end of the school day, my patchy-looking face has got ... a tiny bit ... WORSE.

Because of the audition tonight, Norman  and Derek meet me at the school gate so we can walk back together. They look a bit surprised.

"Don't worry, it will wash off," I tell them.

We go past the audition poster again, which reminds me about Norman's stick-on eyes.

"And those pointy shoes too!" I tell them both.

"What kind of person wears pointy shoes like that?" Derek asks.

"An ALIEN," Norman laughs.

Speaking of shoes – Derek's are still pinching my feet. But I'm not going to worry about that now, because we've only just got enough time to grab something to eat, then get changed. Norman's wearing his T-shirt under his uniform.

"Saves time," he says.

Great – I can tell Dad that DOGZOMBIES are ready to GO!

Mum comes back from work with Delia behind her. She stops – and looks at me.

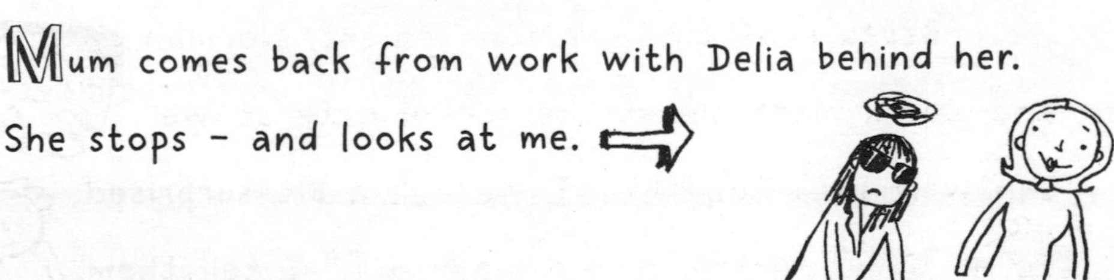

"Have you been using my **fake tan**, Tom?"

"You do look a bit orange, Tom," Derek says.

"The goggle marks are fading, though."

Then Delia **BUTTS** in and says,

"Just call your band The Oompa Loompas and you'll be fine."

"I'm **NOT ORANGE**," I tell Delia. 

"You are a bit, Tom," Mum says. She looks in my swimming bag and brings out what I thought was shampoo. "This is my fake tan – you must have got it on your face!"

There's not enough time to wash it off properly, and Dad says we'll be late if we don't go now.

But Mum shouts,

"Wait ... come here, Tom."

And she only goes and WIPES my face with some kind of cloth.

(It's SO embarrassing.)

mmm
mmm

But most of the fake tan's gone now. I just look a little streaky.

As we're leaving, Delia says, "Even slightly orange, you're still better than those **Nerdy Boys** in jumpers!"

(Which, for Delia, is almost a compliment.)

Dad drives us to the audition, but he's **forgotten** to bring all the right "paperwork" with him. Which means we stand in the wrong queue for a while before anyone notices.

(And we almost miss our audition time.)

I spot the Year Sixes from our school, who are already on stage. "They're good," Derek says.

"I know," I agree.

Dad gives us a "little talk" before it's our turn.

"It's not the end of the world if you don't get through – just do your **BEST**. The standard's pretty high, so don't be disappointed. You'll be fine."

(It's like he doesn't think we've got a chance.)

A lady tells us we're on next. There are drums and keyboards already set up. But we have to wait for the other band to pick up their guitars before we can go on.

While we're waiting, I catch sight of some very **familiar**-looking **pointy shoes...**

"Psssttt." I try and get Derek and Norman's attention.

"Look over there."

Derek is squinting and trying to see.

"**Pointy shoes!**"

I'm making **pointy-shoe** signs with my hands when whoever is behind the curtain suddenly steps out ...

... and WAVES AT US!

(It's only the school inspector in pointy shoes...)

He says, "GOOD LUCK! I saw your name on the audition list. Just thought I'd say HELLO before I have to go back to judging. I used to be a music teacher and a musician before I was an inspector – in case you're wondering."

(He's a JUDGE who wears really pointy shoes.)

"We've got NO chance of getting through the audition NOW, with him as a judge!" I whisper.

"Come on, DOGZOMBIES!" Norman shouts.

I suddenly remember that I brought a pair of shades with me that will hide any goggle marks or fake tan streaks still lurking on my FACE. So I POP them on and walk to the microphone (well, I hobble because of Derek's snug shoes).

"Hello, we're DOGZOMBIES and we're playing 'WILD THING'!" (Here goes...)

We do an OK job of playing the song right up until I have to take off my shades, as I can't see what I'm playing properly - which is a tiny bit awkward.

"Well done, DOGZOMBIES. Thanks for coming and we'll be in touch," the ~~inspector~~ - sorry - the JUDGE says.

And that's it! We're all done, the audition's over. We go to find Dad, who's outside, and guess who's waiting to play next? Only **The Nerdy Boys**, who are wearing BRAND NEW NOVELTY JUMPERS for the occasion.

As we walk past, Norman says, "Nice jumpers."

Dad's waiting and wants to know how we did?

"Well ... apart from my shades being so dark I couldn't see what I was playing, it was OK (sort of)," I say.

We tell Dad about the school inspector being a

(I don't mention 1. me bumping into the inspector

ALL the time

2. me getting caught doodling a

picture of him.

Dad doesn't need to know that.)

I do mention his pointy shoes.

"Imagine if he'd seen you stick those eyes on, Norman!" Derek laughs.

"It was a LUCKY escape there!"

Once we're in the car, Dad says, "I nearly forgot ... your mum suggested that after the audition I could take you to the shops to buy a nice..."

I THINK he's going to say "PAIR OF SENSIBLE SHOES", so I say, "I don't want to go."

I look EXTRA fed up to make a point.

Dad says, "Well, OK, if you really don't want to ...

, that's fine with me."

OF COURSE we want ice cream!

"Your dad's funny," Norman says.

"Hilarious, I know," I say, trying to decide what flavour to have. (Chocolate and caramel, of course.)

The **BAD** news is, **DOGZOMBIES** didn't make it through the **BAND BATTLE** auditions. We're not going to play at the **ROCK WEEKLY** festival. I'm not *THAT* disappointed.

"The more you practice, the better you get," Dad tells me.

(Which sounds like something Uncle Kevin would say.)

But the **GOOD** news is:

Mum found a MUCH better use for those **massive** shoes in the end. She filled them with pebbles and WEDGED them against Delia's door to stop June's cat from sneaking into her room again.

(Rooster's been keeping him away from Derek's house too.)

At school, **AMY** tells me that the Year Six kids didn't get through the auditions either. And they rehearsed LOADS more than we did.

Marcus is still annoying though.

"I heard your audition was a disaster," he tells me.

"It wasn't THAT bad – but we didn't get through."

"I really want to go to the ROCK WEEKLY festival," Marcus says.

"Me too," I say (it's the first time we've agreed about something for AGES).

Mr Fullerman says that our parents will be getting a copy of the SCHOOL INSPECTION REPORT soon.

"Overall the school did very well. There were a few issues with lateness."

I look straight ahead like I don't know what he means.

"But because you all did so well," Mr Fullerman says, **"we can have a screening of the film Mrs Worthington's class did in the hall today."**

HOORAY!

We all cheer.

"And I'll read you the FINAL CHAPTERS of THE VERY SPECIAL RECIPE.**"**

We all cheer again.

HOORAY!

"After our double maths lesson."

SILENCE.

Then Mrs Mumble comes in and asks if she could borrow someone to help her put more chairs out in the hall. MY HAND goes up SO *fast* I get picked straight away.

(AVOID MATHS = RESULT!)

I help Mrs Mumble with the chairs while feeling quite pleased with myself that I've got out of doing maths.

(Genius at work)

I take my time going back into class by dawdling as much as possible,

and when I walk in ...

Mr Fullerman is JUST FINISHING THE STORY!

What?

"Have I missed the ending, sir? I thought we were doing maths?"

"Yes, sorry, Tom, it was my little joke! We did maths the other day. You can take the book out of the library if you want and add it to your reading diary. Which I HOPE you're keeping up to date?"

(Yes, sir. Sort of.)

Marcus says,  "I can tell you the ending."

"NO! I want to read it, don't say anything!" I have to stick my fingers in my ears so I can't hear him. La La La not listening!

Not listening ... he's stopped.

If I fill in the last few pages of my reading diary myself, I'll be able to get a brand new one.

Then Mum or Dad can start signing it again.

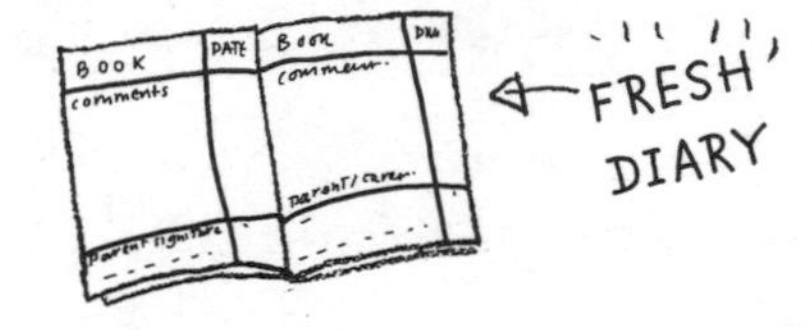

Mr Fullerman lets me go to the library at lunchtime so I can take out the book and read the ending. ☺

But when I get there and try to find it, Miss Page, the librarian, says someone's just taken it out. "Already?"

"Yes – it's that boy there. He said he wanted to read it again. He might let you read it first if you ask him?" she tells me. But when I see who it is ...

... why bother? He'll only say no. Or **tell** me the ending. (Or both.)

I'll just have to wait until he's read the WHOLE book (again). Groan.

I'm about to go to lunch when Miss Page runs over and says, "It's your **lucky day**, Tom!" She's only found another copy of the book. **YES!** I'll get to read the ending after all (despite Marcus).

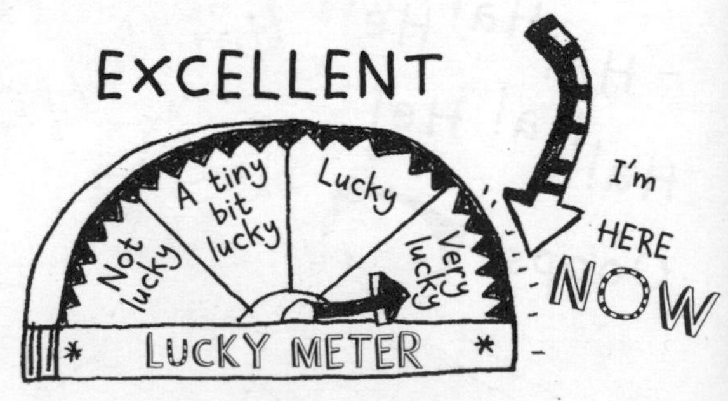

I take a quick look at the last page in the book (I can't help myself). Then I pop it in my bag to read later at home.

But the highlight of the WHOLE day has to be watching the film that Derek's class made. We watch it in the hall and I don't think I've EVER heard the school LAUGH that loudly before.

Solid was LAUGHING so much he nearly squashed me.

(This is what made us laugh the most...)

Mrs Worthington's EXTREME ALIEN close-up!

(So funny.)

AND I still have MY BOOK to read! But avoiding Marcus is getting tricky. He keeps RUSHING up to me and trying to tell me the ending.

"The bit with the BUGS is really good. It all finishes with..."

"HEY, MARCUS!" I say to stop him.

"Remember this? EEEEEEEEWWWWWWWW bugs!"

Which shuts him up for a while.

I ignore him as much as I can until the bell goes.

When I get home, I manage to watch a bit of THE CRAZY FRUIT BUNCH first.

Then I fill in my reading diary (and sign it).

Then I really impress Mum by casually mentioning that I'm going to bed EARLY so I can read my book.

Sigh...

Now, where was I –

Mayor Bottle arrives at the tea shop...

"Good afternoon, Mayor, I'm so glad you could join us," Mrs Crumble said. She tried to shake the mayor's hand but he ignored her and walked into the shop.

A food inspector took Mrs Crumble's hand but didn't shake it. Instead he dabbed it with a cotton bud and placed the bud in a sealed pot for testing.

"Start as we mean to go on," the mayor said coldly. Mrs Crumble looked surprised.

"It's a SHAME we HAVE to do this inspection on YOUR TEA SHOP. But SOMEONE reported there were bugs and cockroaches around THIS area – and we can't be too careful, can we?"

"I'm sure you won't find anything like that here," Mr Crumble told him.

"This could all be avoided if you change your mind about moving out?" the mayor added.

"This TEA SHOP is not going anywhere and neither are we," Mrs Crumble told him.

"We'll see about that," the mayor said, taking a seat at one of the tables. **"Shall we get started?"** he said, then waved his hand at the inspectors, who began to pull on their rubber gloves.

Walter's inspection team started in the tea room. They DABBED, SWABBED and SCRAPED everywhere they could reach. Roger's team went to the kitchen. They looked through fridges, pots, pans, dishes, and right into the oven that was still warm from baking brownies. The Crumble family watched them closely and tried to stay calm.

Mr Crumble approached the mayor and VERY politely asked him, **"As this is going to take a while, Mayor, could I possibly TEMPT you to try a hot chocolate with maybe a lovely warm sticky brownie?"** He lifted up a PLATE of the brownies and wafted them under the mayor's nose so he could smell how fresh they were and the mayor's hair began to MOVE slowly on its own.

Cocoa
powder

"I'm not expecting to be here for very long," the mayor said, looking at the brownies. They did smell good and he was quite hungry. **"They'll be closed soon enough, so why not. Yes, pass them here,"** he muttered as he helped himself to a brownie. It was rich and sticky, cut into a square and dusted with icing sugar.

Then Mr Crumble went to make the mayor a hot chocolate. He stirred some of his special ready-grated chocolate into the warm milk, then poured it into a bowl to froth up. Mr Crumble ladled the thick, delicious chocolatey mixture into a mug. He checked that everything was perfect and stirred it some more (a lot more than usual) ... just in case.

"Would you like one marshmallow or two with your hot chocolate?" Mr Crumble asked.

"Try three," the mayor told him greedily. **"And another brownie too."**

The mayor sat at the table and enjoyed being waited on. With one SLURP all three marshmallows disappeared. He bit into the brownie. **"Mmmmmmmmm, that's not bad. Do you have a special recipe for these?"** he wanted to know.

Mrs Crumble coughed. **"Errr, yes, Mayor, we do. We have a special ingredient that we like to keep secret."**

"When THE TEA SHOP is closed you must give me the recipe." He laughed with his mouth full.

The Crumble family watched him eat and said nothing.

CHAPTER 4

The inspectors continued to work while the mayor ate his treats. So far they'd found NOTHING. Not one single little SIGN that any bugs had ever been there.

Walter and Roger were beginning to wonder how this could have happened.

"It was the right shop we went to last night, wasn't it?" Walter whispered to Roger.

"YES OF COURSE IT WAS! I poured the bugs down the pipe myself, I should know!"

"If this doesn't work, we'll have to go to PLAN B," Walter whispered again.

"What's PLAN B?" Roger wondered.

"You did bring a PLAN B with you?" Walter could tell from Roger's face that he'd forgotten to bring a PLAN B.

Plan B stood for Plan BUG, which was to bring SPARE bugs and drop them around when no one was looking.

"We could try plan C?" Roger whispered.

"What's plan C?" Walter wanted to know.

"We CRY and hope the mayor feels sorry for us?"

Walter muttered **"Idiot"** under his breath and carried on searching for something that resembled a tiny mouse dropping or two.

The mayor had helped himself to YET another brownie and finished off the last of his hot chocolate. He was getting impatient and wanted to know WHAT was going on. **"This tea and cake STUFF is all very nice but what I really want to know is ... HAVE YOU FOUND ANYTHING YET?"**

No one said a word.

Until one inspector held up a SOCK. **"I've found this under the counter."**

"I've been looking for that!" Plum told him and took it back.

"Never mind THAT - WHERE ARE THE COCKROACHES?" the mayor bellowed.

"Well ... so far, Mayor ... there's ... no sign of any bugs or pests," Roger said.

"BUT we're still looking," Walter told the mayor.

Sock?

The mayor's face turned purple with **RAGE**.

(AND he'd had a bit too much sugar.)

He looked like he was about to EXPLODE.

"THERE MUST be something here – you promised me there would be. THAT WAS THE PLAN!" he shouted at Walter.

The inspectors lined up and shook their heads, as NEITHER of them had found a single trace of a bug, mouse, rat or cockroach in THE TEA SHOP.

Mr Crumble interrupted. **"Does that mean we've passed the inspection, then, Mr Mayor?"**

The mayor stood up and pushed away the table.

"Listen, CRUMBLE, don't you think you've got away with THIS. I'll find a way to BUILD my tower RIGHT HERE."

He stomped his foot and the squirrel on his head opened its EYES. It was hard for Apple and Plum not to STARE at his head.

Mrs Crumble tried to calm everyone down by saying, **"It would be SUCH a shame to let all these good cakes go to waste. If you're leaving, let me give you them to take with you."**

The inspectors all nodded in agreement, then looked at the mayor. Mr Crumble handed the mayor a LARGE box of brownies that were tied up with a ribbon. **"No hard feelings, Mayor. Take the box home with you and eat them later."**

The Mayor SNATCHED the brownies (he did like them, after all), then spun round angrily and said, **"I don't know what you've done or how you've done it – BUT somewhere in this TEA SHOP there must be ONE TINY BUG or even a rodent of some kind. And when I FIND IT, your TEA SHOP will be closed down for GOOD!"**

The mayor's HAIR began to MOVE as he shouted.

Apple and Plum started to laugh.

"Listen, KIDDIES - you might be laughing now, but when this place is GONE and you have nowhere to LIVE, then you'll be SORRY," the vile mayor told them.

The inspectors were trying not to laugh too. The squirel's tail had slipped down over the mayor's face. Plum pointed to the mayor's head and said, **"Mr Mayor, is that a SQUIRREL on top of your head?"** Everyone went silent.

"Look, there it is peeking out!" Plum laughed again.

The MAYOR was FURIOUS! How DARE they mention his hair.

He flew into a **RAGE** and stormed out of THE TEA SHOP – and right into the press, where all the photographers took hundreds of pictures of him looking STARTLED with a squirrel on top of his head.

The inspectors left the shop, happily taking all the cakes and brownies they could eat with them. **"We can't keep them – have as many as you want!"** Mr Crumble handed Walter and Roger a box each too, which they gratefully took away.

"We must have got the wrong building – it's the only answer," Walter said as he left THE TEA SHOP. They both knew they would be in trouble with the mayor.

They'd worry about that later.

The the whole Crumble family breathed a BIG sigh of relief, then cheered!

They shut the TEA-SHOP door and turned the sign to CLOSED. **"We did it!"**

THE TEA SHOP was SAFE and still open for business.

And would remain open for quite some time to come.

CHAPTER 5

BUT – that's not quite the end of the story...

If you've been paying CLOSE attention, you've probably already GUESSED what happened to the bugs and vermin that invaded THE TEA SHOP.

If you haven't ...

SPOILER ALERT!

I'm going to tell you anyway.

The FIRST thing Mr Crumble did was TRAP all the mice and the rats in boxes, using cakes as BAIT. Then he sealed them up and posted them back to the food inspectors' offices.

And as for the BUGS, let's just say that the secret recipe Mrs Crumble was talking about for the brownies? You won't find it in ANY cookbook **ever.**

But just for you ... here it is.

SPECIAL BROWNIE RECIPE

185g unsalted butter

185g best dark chocolate

85g plain flour

40g cocoa powder

50g white chocolate

3 large eggs

275g golden caster sugar

And if you're wondering what happened to Mayor Cuthbert Banjo Baby Bottle, you can read all about it in the papers.

Because after the pictures of him appeared with a SQUIRREL nestling on his head ...

… a "close friend" let slip how the mayor had tried to force THE TEA SHOP out of business so he could buy the land for his TOWER. No one likes a bully, and at the next election, he was voted out of office.

Thankfully THE TEA SHOP is still there and THRIVING, and still making delicious cakes and bread (but WITHOUT any extra ingredients).

The tower was never built and Mayor Bottle (who is currently waiting for a hair transplant) lives with his pet squirrel at the top of a block of flats. Which is as near as he is EVER going to get to Bottle Towers.

There were LOADS of other things that happened too. But we'll have to save that for another story.

(for now).

SPECIAL
RECIPE

Book Title

Date

The Very Special Recipe

I REALLY liked this book. It had LOTS of disgusting bugs in it and a NASTY mayor. It was funny too.

It was a GOOD story with a TWIST at the end (yuck).

AND all the bugs reminded me of when Marcus thought he'd eaten some bugs on his PIZZA. THAT was funny.

The pictures were good too.

Parent's/Carer's comments and signature

Date

Tom has done well.

We think he's a ~~genius~~ smart.

There, all done - the book is finished and my READING DIARY is now UP TO DATE.

Hopefully Mr Fullerman will say I can get a new DIARY now.

And he WON'T notice the "EXTRA" bits I've added.

(If I'm LUCKY.)

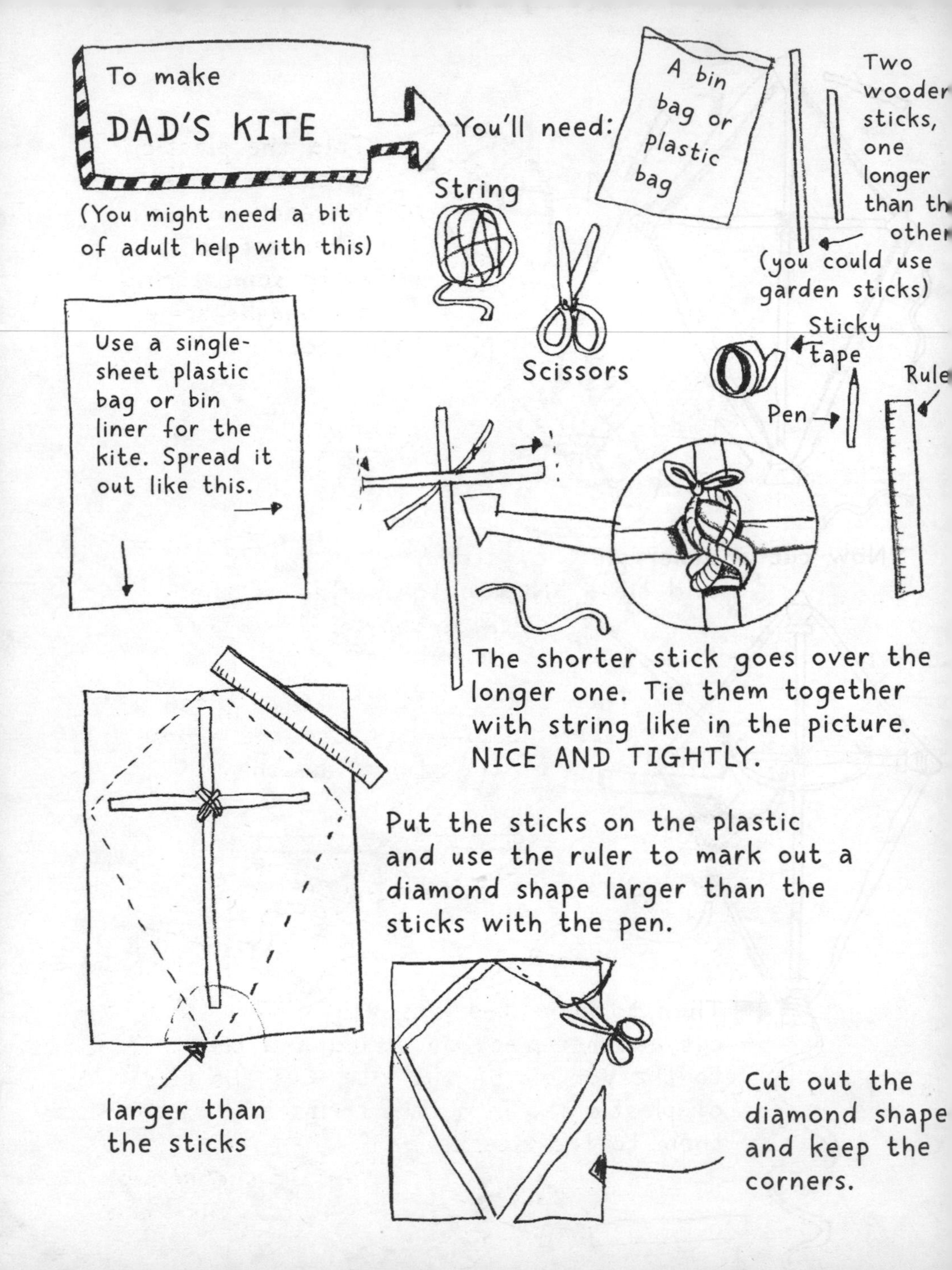
To make
DAD'S KITE
You'll need:
(You might need a bit of adult help with this)
A bin bag or plastic bag
Two wooden sticks, one longer than the other
(you could use garden sticks)
String
Scissors
Sticky tape
Pen
Ruler
Use a single-sheet plastic bag or bin liner for the kite. Spread it out like this.
The shorter stick goes over the longer one. Tie them together with string like in the picture. NICE AND TIGHTLY.
Put the sticks on the plastic and use the ruler to mark out a diamond shape larger than the sticks with the pen.
larger than the sticks
Cut out the diamond shape and keep the corners.

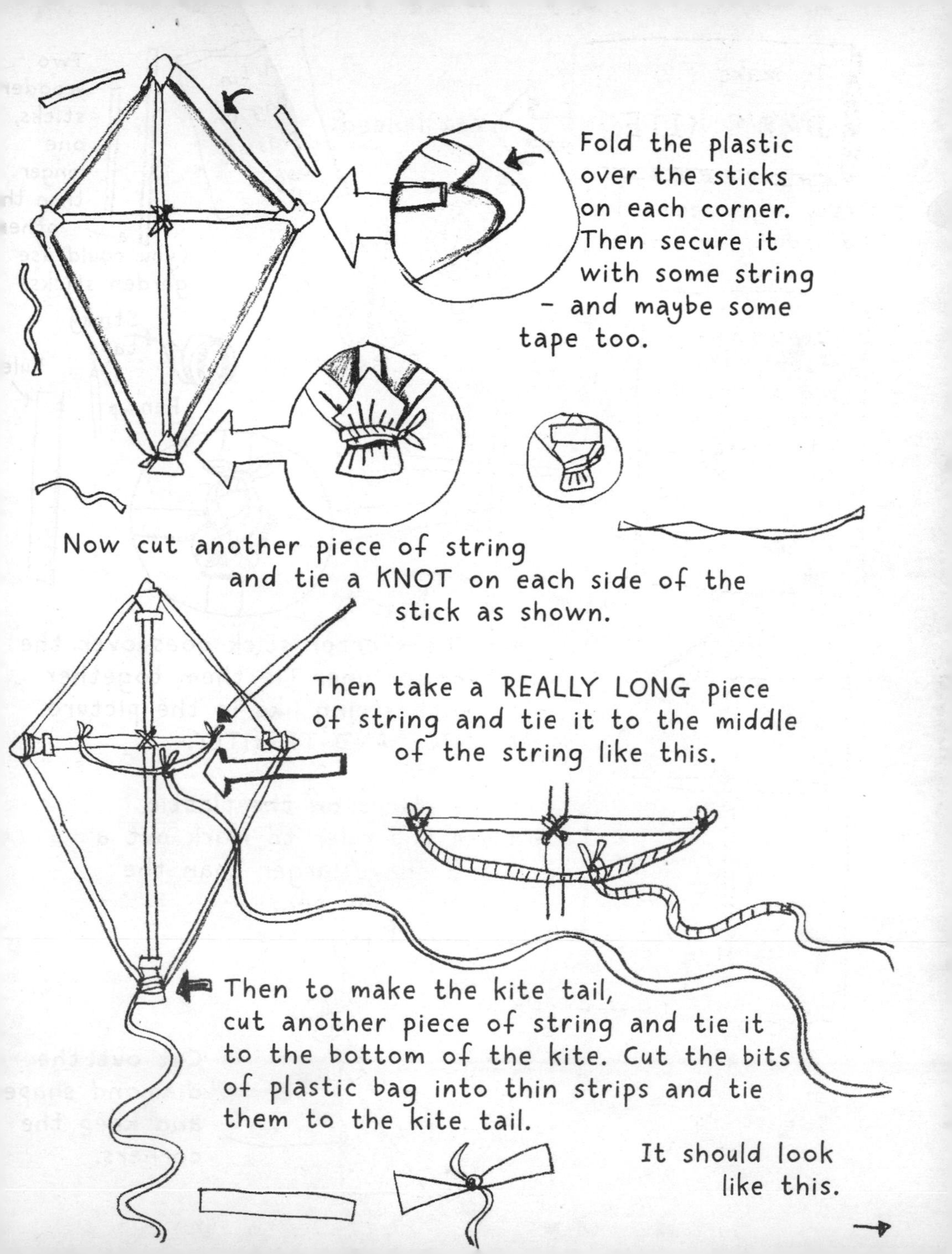
Fold the plastic over the sticks on each corner. Then secure it with some string – and maybe some tape too.
Now cut another piece of string and tie a KNOT on each side of the stick as shown.
Then take a REALLY LONG piece of string and tie it to the middle of the string like this.
Then to make the kite tail, cut another piece of string and tie it to the bottom of the kite. Cut the bits of plastic bag into thin strips and tie them to the kite tail.
It should look like this.

And HERE'S YOUR FINISHED KITE, ready for some FRESH AIR and some FLYING... (If you're lucky.)

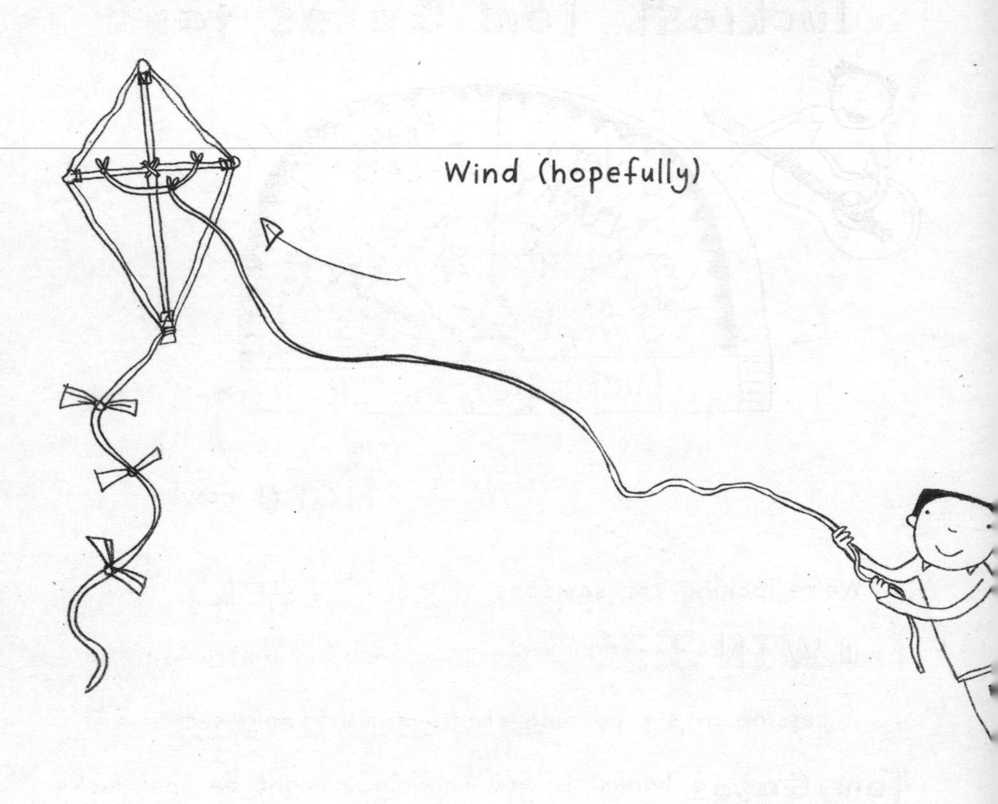

Are YOU the UK's luckiest Tom Gates fan?

Here now!

We're looking for someone VERY LUCKY who will WIN £300 worth of musical instruments, a session in a recording studio and a whole set of Tom Gates books! If you think you might be that lucky someone, head to www.scholastic.co.uk/tomgatesworld and enter the free Tom Gates lucky competition.

We also have 12 prizes for runners-up, so if you're just a TINY BIT LUCKY you might win one of those.

GOOD LUCK!

Love Tom Gates?

Why not visit his

BRILLIANT, Excellent, AMAZING, Genius, FANTASTIC

and

Extra Special

WEBSITE at

www.scholastic.co.uk/tomgatesworld

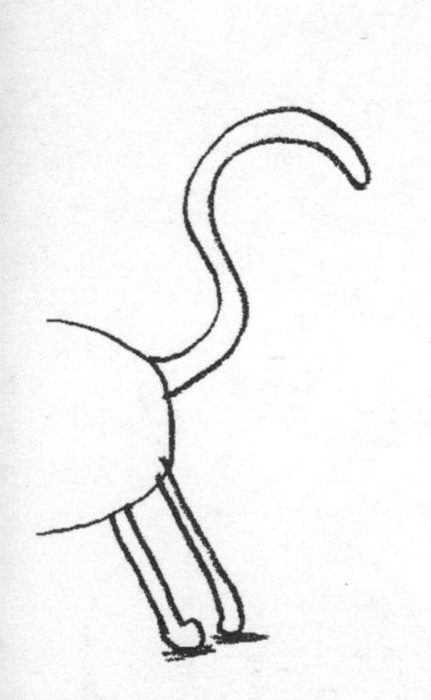

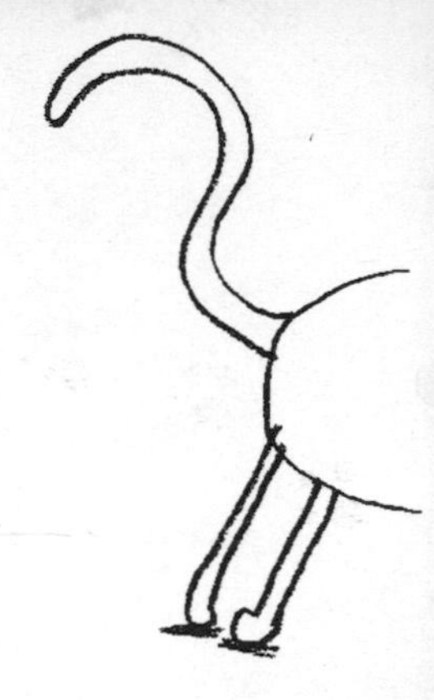

Explore Tom's world

Test your knowledge

of Tom's family, friends and teachers

Enter competitions

Play games like "Scribble School"

Download brilliant activity sheets

Upload your own doodles

Take the daily challenge

Sign up to the Tom Gates newsletter

Meet Liz and find out about all her books

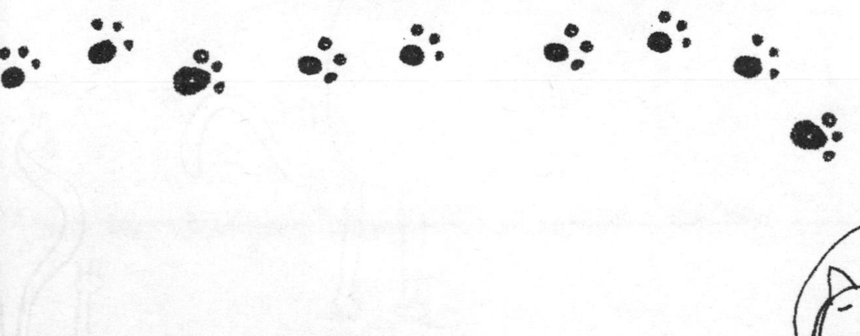

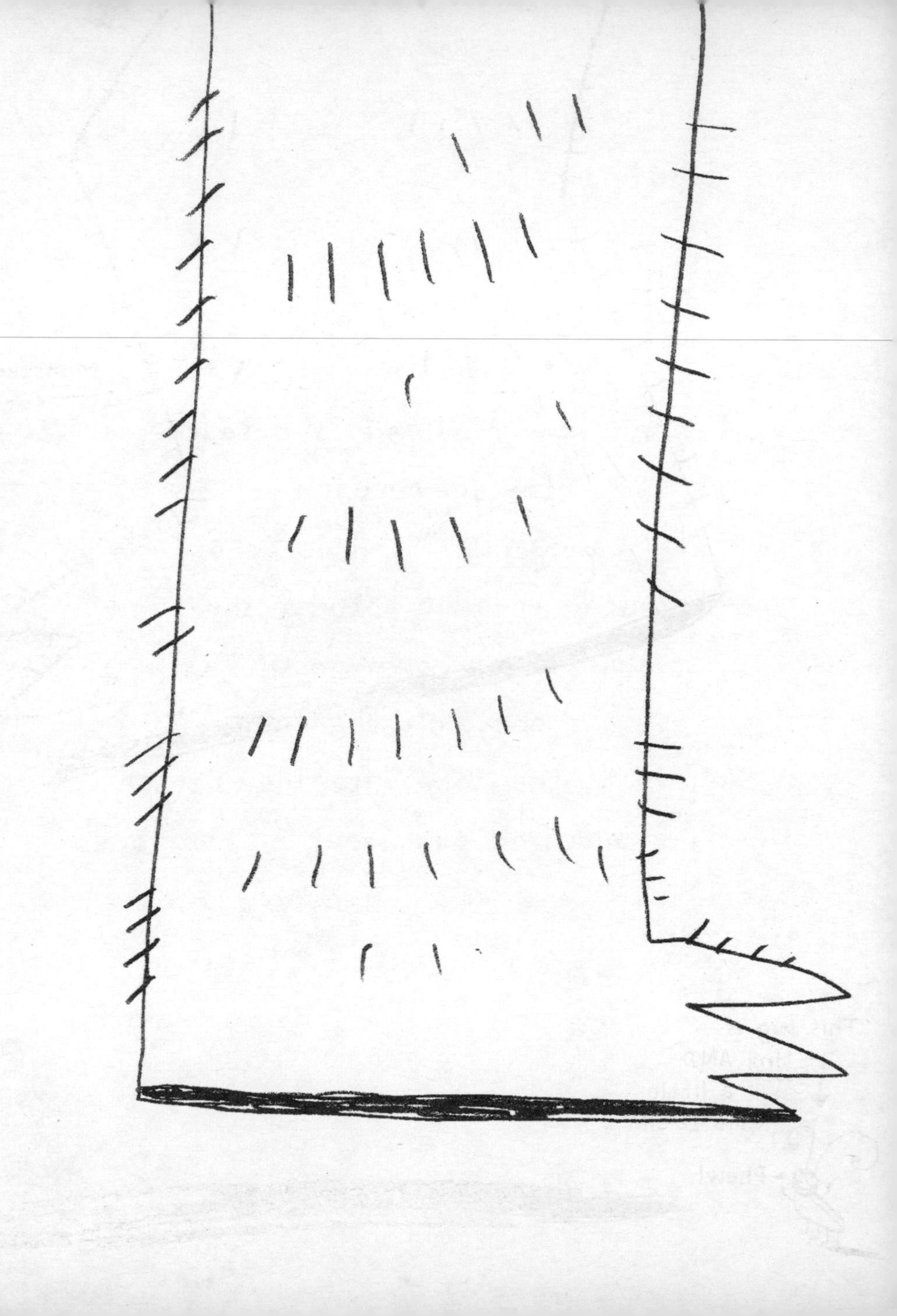

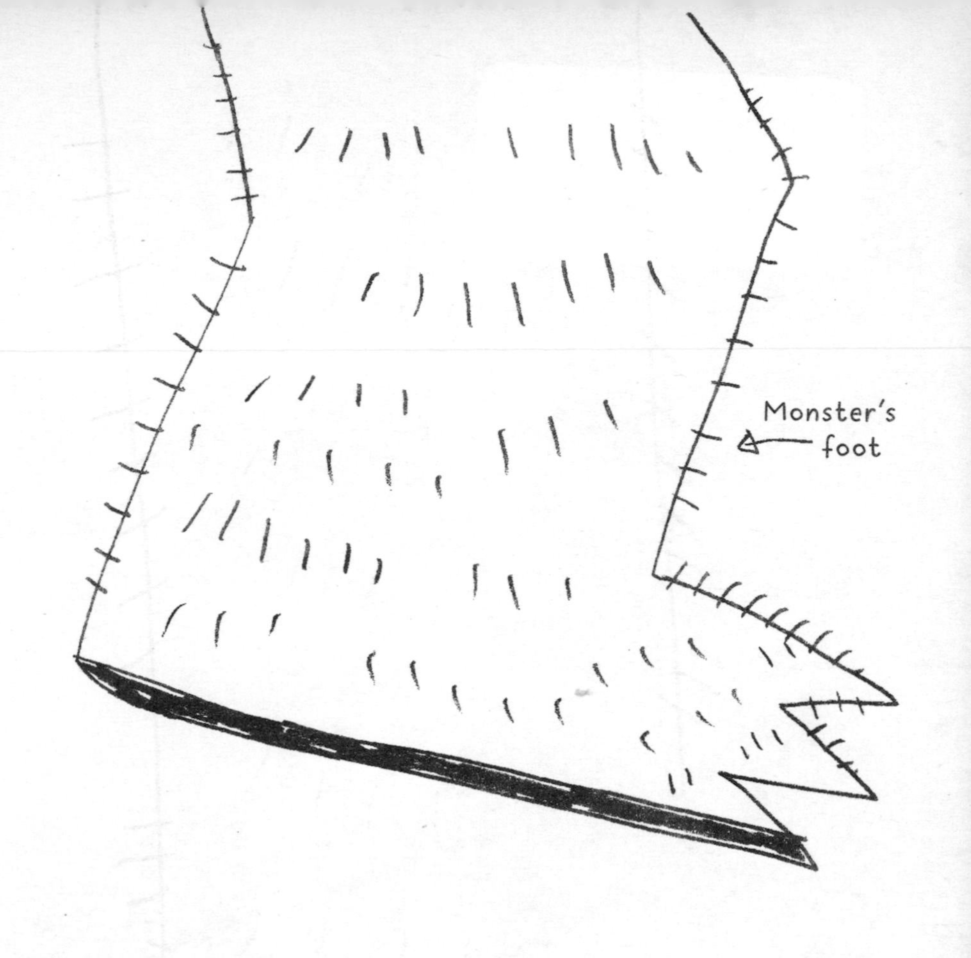

This bug is
tiny AND
a little
bit LUCKY

Phew!

cat book barrier

TOM GATES
IS ABSOLUTELY FANTASTIC
(at SOME things)
By L. Pichon
TOM GATES
EXTRA SPECIAL TREATS (not)
BY L. Pichon

WINNER OF THE ROALD DAHL FUNNY PRIZE 2011
The Brilliant world of
TOM GATES
READ it
BY L. Pichon

TOM GATES
Excellent Excuses
(and other good stuff)
By L. Pichon
Brilliant!

TOM GATES
Everything's AMAZING
(sort of)
By L. Pichon

TOM GATES
GENIUS IDEAS
(mostly)
By L. Pichon